# ONESIMUS

## Also by Bill Spencer

*The Thrilling Adventures of King David*
*Reach Higher* (out of print)
*The Greatest Secret* (out of print)

# BILL SPENCER

# ⊙NESIMUS

## THE FORGIVEN FUGITIVE

gatekeeper press

Published in the United States of America

ISBN: 9781642370157
Fiction / Christian / Historical
14.10.09

This book is lovingly dedicated to
my two precious children, Mark and Cindy

# Acknowledgements

The author wishes to express his appreciation for additional research found in Smith's Bible Dictionary, compiled by William Smith, published by A.J. Holman Company.

The original Josephus Complete Works, translated from original Greek language. American Imprint Collection Library of Congress, First Century AD.

God's Warrior by Frank Slaughter, published by Doubleday and Company, Inc.

MacArthur Study Bible by John MacArthur, published by Thomas Nelson.

# Author's Note

To those who read this book, it is my sincere prayer that the times, the places, and the people of the First Christian Century may come alive for them as they have for me. And that they, too, may come to know Jesus, the risen Lord, as did my friend Onesimus, the forgiven fugitive.

# CONTENTS

Part I   Rome 64–68 AD ....................................................... 13

  1 ............................................................................. 15

  2 ............................................................................. 26

  3 ............................................................................. 33

  4 ............................................................................. 38

  5 ............................................................................. 44

Part II   The Evil Tribune ............................................... 53

  6 ............................................................................. 55

  7 ............................................................................. 63

  8 ............................................................................. 67

  9 ............................................................................. 74

  10 ........................................................................... 82

  11 ........................................................................... 87

  12 ........................................................................... 92

  13 ......................................................................... 100

  14 ......................................................................... 106

  15 ......................................................................... 111

  16 ......................................................................... 118

Part III     Alexandria.................................................... 125

    17 ................................................................ 127

    18 ................................................................ 131

    19 ................................................................ 137

    20 ................................................................ 144

    21 ................................................................ 151

    22 ................................................................ 160

Part IV     Rome: The Arena Miracle ..................... 163

    23 ................................................................ 165

    24 ................................................................ 170

    25 ................................................................ 174

Part V     Colosse: The Forgiven Fugitive ............. 181

    26 ................................................................ 183

    27 ................................................................ 188

    28 ................................................................ 193

    29 ................................................................ 195

A Closing Word ................................................. 197

# PART I

# ROME 64–68 AD

# 1

Onesimus was awakened at dawn by the shout of an officer as they approached the mainland of Italy. The galley slaves of the Alexandrian vessel Castor and Pollux were pulling steadily in the rhythm beaten out upon a small drum by a shipmate. An overseer trod the narrow walkway along the center of the vessel, ready to lay his long whip across the shoulders of any oarsman who might falter in the rhythm, threatening to entangle the long sweeps and throw the ship off course.

Each galley slave was chained to the great oar that he pulled. If one oar failed to move in cadence with the others, the whip cracked and there was the scream of pain. Scars from the whip showed upon the backs of the slaves, even though their skin had long since been burned almost black by the sun, while here and there, the stain of blood betrayed a more recent whipping.

It was still winter, though already warm here in the southern part of Italy. They had sailed to Syracuse, then Rheqium, and finally almost directly northward to Puteoli, the major harbor serving the bustling city of Neapolis. Across the bay the buildings of Puteoli were now visible, rising in gradual ascent from the waterfront. A point of land to the north hid Baie, the famous watering place of Roman nobility and playground of the emperors.

Through dark expressive eyes, Onesimus could see the waterfront was jammed with ships of all sizes. He glanced around at others who were now waking up. Some were slaves, others were freedmen, such as he had hoped to be, a promise made to him by his master Philemon when his mother died. Now that promise may never be realized.

A serious expression came across his handsome face marked by maturity far beyond his twenty-one years of age. As a slave, hard labor had been his lot most of his life. Raised by Greek parents in Phrygia, he had spent most of his teenage years working in the silver mines. A mine accident killed his father and two other men. At the request of his mother, the owner of the mine released Onesimus from his duty in the mines. Shortly after the death of his father, he and his mother were sold to a rich Greek merchant traveling through Phrygia on his way to Colosse. However, his mother became ill and died shortly after their move.

Onesimus suddenly felt alone in the world. His master Philemon and his wife Apphia were good to him. His job was working in the vineyards along with their son Archippus, who was the same age of Onesimus.

On the first day of each week, friends from around Colosse would gather at his master's house to worship a Jesus Christ whom Onesimus did not fully understand. It was the first exposure he had of Christianity. They claimed Jesus was crucified and rose from the dead. Some said they were eye witnesses and saw him after his resurrection. They would talk of his return to earth to rule and reign from Jerusalem. It was all confusing and strange to Onesimus. They also spoke of one whose name is Paul who converted Philemon and his family to Christianity, but was now a prisoner in Rome awaiting trial before the Roman Court.

With the approval of Philemon, Onesimus spent much of his free time at the library in Colosse, which was located in the temple of Zeus and was flanked on the sides by two stories of library scrolls. Over one hundred thousand scrolls were found here on virtually every subject and on every country. He had studied hard and read much.

His desire in life had been to travel, and now that dream was being realized. However, his leaving Colosse was not without a sense of guilt. He had not told Philemon that he was leaving. Philemon had been like a father to him, and it would have been difficult to face him. He only hoped that he would not be blamed for the money that Archippus had stolen from his father's strong box. Onesimus was fearful that when Philemon found the money missing, Archippus would falsely accuse him of stealing the money.

Onesimus had very little savings, enough, however, to purchase passage on a ship bound for Rome, a place he had always wanted to go. And so he left Colosse at night and traveled south to Myra where he caught a ship. This vessel which was laden with grain had left Alexandria bound for Rome. Myra was its first stop. Here the current sets westward toward Rome.

Loud shouts brought Onesimus back to the present. The captain of the ship was giving an order, and the galley slaves on the eastward side banked their oars. The great vessel swung sharply, thrusting its prow into a narrow passage between rocks jutting out of the sea and the end of the great stone water breaker on the left. From the huge swells of the sea, the ship shot through the opening into the glassy waters of the harbor itself.

Onesimus had read much about this major harbor which served the bustling city of Neapolis. Nervously, he anticipated what he might see and experience in the months ahead.

The ship was coming into the quay at Puteoli now: the slaves on the side of the vessel nearest the dock had already drawn in their sweeps and placed them upon the deck against the rail. Those on the opposite side were now manipulating their oars under the direction of an overseer, moving blades back and forth in the water to propel the ship sideways. When it bumped gently against the quay, ropes were tossed from the deck and secured to bollards.

Orders were given and the group of slaves not occupied with, the oars took up the gangplank which, while underway, was secured against the rail, acting both as cushions for breakwater that sweep over the deck in a storm, and as a means of departure from the vessel. The gangplank was finally made secure and ready for passengers and cargo to depart.

The quays were thronged with people, sailors, soldiers, merchants shouting their wares, wine sellers with bulbous wine skins on their backs, beggars of every nationality, brilliant-colored clothing from every country of the world—all crowded the docks.

Onesimus stopped in astonishment. He was not prepared for what he saw. The crowded quay was teeming with unattached women of every nationality, every color, every social level. A haughty Roman wife walked idly along in her finery, attended by a coal-black slave girl naked above the snow-white cloth wrapped about her body as a skirt. A courtesan ambled by smiling at Onesimus, cheeks painted with antimony, eyelids dripping with kohl, lips vivid with carmine, with an inviting gaze. Dark-skinned Egyptian girls walked with blond descendants of the soldiers brought here by the legion of Caesar. It seemed to Onesimus that there were more courtesans in Puteoli than respectable women, which was not far from the truth.

He knew that in a Jewish community, these painted women would have been stoned by an outraged populace, but although Onesimus instinctively turned his head at the sight of them, he could not entirely still the quickening of his pulse at the sight of lovely bodies half revealed by draperies cunningly arranged so as to leave one beautiful breast entirely bare. Lest he find temptation stronger than his will, Onesimus turned to the quays themselves where the work of loading and unloading ships went on both night and day.

All the produce which men traded the world over lay on the massive wharves of this great sea port, where no custom fees were charged on goods shipped to other destinations. Silken cloth and cheaper cotton fabric from the far-distant domain of the Han emperors, apes, peacocks, and precious jewels from the ports of Malabar; spices and precious incense from the cities of Arabia; ivory and gold from the land of the blacks called Nubia—these and hundreds of other goods filled the quays and the great warehouses. Long lines of slaves marched up and down the gang planks under the whip of the overseers, handling cargo even at night. From the bottomless granary of the Nile Valley flowed an endless stream of grain for Rome and its soldiers.

Anxious to reach the capital city, which he thought would take a couple of days, he made his way through the noisy crowded docks, through Puteoli to Capua where he picked up the Appian Way. Here the traffic increased markedly, since this was one of the great roadways of the empire. More than once, he and others were forced to leave the stone-paved road and walk beside it, while an elaborate curtained palanquim passed, born by burly slaves. And occasionally, the rumbling wheels of a heavy carriage, loaded with the family and possessions of some nobleman, could be felt upon the stone pavement well before its appearance.

North of Anxur, the road descended from the hills back of the seashore to follow the bank of the canal by which Augustus had drained the Pontine marshes. The canal ended at the Appii Forum. As darkness fell, Onesimus and others turned aside to spend the night. He made friends with two young men who made their bedrolls near him. These young men he judged to be Jews from their appearance, perhaps in their twenties.

"I am Timothy from Galatia, and this is John Mark from Asia," the young man volunteered.

Onesimus, reluctant to reveal much about himself, replied simply, "I am Onesimus from Perga," as he pulled out a chunk of dried fruit from his bag of belongings.

"We are going to Rome to deliver some things that a friend of ours requested. What brings you to Rome, Onesimus?" Timothy asked.

"I, ah, I thought I might find work there," he stammered.

"As big and as strong as you look to be, I'm sure you will have no problem finding something," Mark stated.

Their journey continued early the next morning. Strung out behind Onesimus and his two friends, trudged a host of people. After several hours of walking, they came to Three Taverns where they spent the second night.

"We have friends in Aricia which is just outside Rome. It will be difficult to find a place to stay in Rome, especially after dark. Mark and I plan to spend the night with them. I'm sure you would be welcome, too," invited Timothy.

"Thank you, I appreciate your offer," replied Onesimus.

It was late in the afternoon when they reached Aricia, and Mark and Timothy were overjoyed when they saw Aquila and Priscilla—whom they had last seen at Ephesus. The couple were tent makers who lived in Rome and had come to Aricia to visit friends. After introducing Onesimus, they ate food prepared for them, and after a night's rest, they headed toward Rome. Aquila and Priscilla would show the two young men where the Apostle Paul lived.

From Aricia, it would be an easy walk to the Roman capital. Not far beyond Aricia, Onesimus had his first glimpse of Rome. At the summit of a hill, he climbed upon a rock, the better to see the city. Beyond Aricia, the road descended steadily for a walk of about two hours. At the Porta Capena in the ancient wall, they passed beneath an arch where water dripped constantly from the aqueduct passing over it.

Moving onward, they came to what was known as the Sacra Via, the street leading to the center of the imperial government in Rome. Here at the Milliarium Aureum was located, the golden milestone from which all roads of the empire originated. In front of it was the famous Capitoline Hill upon which stood the house of Caesar and, beside that, the praetorium of the elite guards. Presided over by General Afranius Burrus, one of the bravest and most respected generals in Rome, the praetorium also housed the central prison for the empire, where those awaiting verdict by the imperial courts were held.

As Onesimus followed the Christian group down the street, to his ears came the voice of a young woman singing in purist Greek, soft, sweet, gentle, and clear, with a quality that held him spellbound. He listened and then made his way down the street. Turning a corner, Onesimus came into the open square before a forum. A crowd had gathered there and was still applauding the singer, showering coins at her feet as tokens of their praise.

Onesimus leaned against a pillar supporting the Roman forum. From that vantage point, he could see the singer holding a lyre against her breast. The crowd, largely Greeks and Romans, was arranged around her in a semi-circle. She was young, perhaps eighteen, Onesimus thought, and tall for a Jewish woman. Although her body was slender, it was already filled out with the promise of womanly beauty that could not be denied. Her hair was covered by a shawl, as was the custom of Jewish women in the open air, but no mere fabric could hide its lustrous beauty. As red as the copper dug and refined from the mines of King Solomon at Ezion Gaber. It shone in the late afternoon sunlight, framing her face in a halo of rich color.

The girl's features were a mixture of Hebrew and Greek lines, the cheek bones were moderately prominent, the chin pointed slightly, a classic beauty. Her deep-violet eyes searched the crowd now, as if she were estimating just how many more coins could be extracted from the men applauding her so vigorously. She responded with a warm smile to the encouragement of the crowd.

She was brave, thought Onesimus, daring to sing a love song before a crowd like this in a city shunned and cursed by Jews. Though her dress was clean and beautifully made, it was worn and frayed, as was the leather of the sandals upon here lovely slender feet.

The four musicians with the girl seemed to be Nabateans for their skin was dark and their profiles sharp and hawk like. Their dress, too, was the long flowing robe worn by the sons of the desert who roamed the sandy wastes to the south and east of the Jordan River and the Dead Sea, where lay the great city of Petra. The leader, taller than the others and with a striking face and graying beard, held a large cithara in his hands.

One of the other dark-faced musicians held a long pipe of Egyptian reed and another a trumpet of brass. A fourth carried cymbals strapped to his hands, and upon his feet were the resonant boards called scabella, which were stamped in rhythm to the melody. It was an odd group, but such bands were not uncommon in the thriving populous cities, but Onesimus did not remember one before with a girl singer whose voice was itself a more perfect instrument than those of the musicians and whose beauty made her stand out like a rose among thorns.

"Who is she?" Onesimus asked a Roman who was standing near by, a fat man in a grease-stained toga threatening to burst at the seams.

The Roman looked at him scathingly, as if it were a sacrilege for a foreigner in a cheap robe to speak to his betters. "She is called Leah of Petra," he volunteered grudgingly. "A meretrix, no doubt."

Onesimus knew the Roman word. The meretrix, or prostitute, was common wherever Romans gathered, and women entertainers usually came from this class. Devout Jews applied the word "Jezebel" indiscriminately to the women of their Roman conquerors.

But to Onesimus, the girl from Petra did not look like one of the women of the streets. No paint or antimony whitened the translucent pallor of her skin. Nor could the henna of Cleopatra's Egypt have added anything to the natural luster of her hair. She was beautiful enough to be a courtesan, it was true, but something about her manner, notably the quiet dignity with which she sat there holding the lyre and accepting the plaudits of the crowd, told a different story.

"More! more!" the crowd began to chant now, and others took up the cry.

Leah of Petra smiled and drew her fingers across the lyre, drawing a melody from the strings like the soft murmur of water flowing over rocks in some hidden place of beauty. Then she began to sing a love song, and Onesimus wondered how she had learned her skill on the lyre, but never, he was sure, had it been sung by so beautiful a voice, not even in the palace of a king.

While she was singing, Onesimus looked over the crowd. Only a few were Jews including his new friends. Most were from other parts of the world. They had come eagerly, for much gold could be earned, or stolen, while serving the Romans whose pleasure villas lined the banks of the Tiber River that flowed through Rome. These elaborate villas, with terraced green lawns enclosed by high masonry walls and graceful marble stairways descending to the waters edge, where ornate barges awaited their master's pleasure.

All the emotions of man were betrayed in the eyes of those watching the girl. Some were lost in the beauty of her voice, the fluid notes of the lyre, and the contact with the sublime that beautiful music can bring to those who love it. Others had forgotten the music in admiring the youth and loveliness of the singer. But in a few burned only a fire of lust for the slender body of the girl, and the most notable of these was a Roman officer standing to one side.

He wore the purple-dyed uniform of a tribune. He was tall, with handsome classic features. Domitian was the son of Vespasian and the commander of Nero's personal troops. Already the whole region buzzed with tales of the cruelty of this hated Roman to those who were unfortunate to come under his hands. His fondness for the wine cup and women, and the orgies and revels that were often held at his villa were scandalous in there abandonment. Onesimus noticed that Leah's singing was directed toward the Roman.

The song ended and the musicians lifted their instruments. Then with a crashing chord from the leader's cithara, they began a wild barbaric dance of the mountains and deserts beyond the Jordan River and the Dead Sea. The flute wailed in the strange melody of the desert people, while the strings and the cymbalist took up the rhythm, set to the throbbing beat of the scabella. Stamped by the symbol player against the stones of the pavement, the resonate boards produced a booming sound like the beat of a drum heard afar off. Above this heady rhythm came the clear, commanding call of the lone trumpet.

The music seemed to caress Leah's body as she stood erect upon her toes, poised with her arms uplifted, as if in adoration of something unseen. The music created a fluid rhythm in cadence with the clash of cymbals, the throbbing beat of the scabella and the strings, and the wail of the flute and trumpet. Slowly at first, then faster as the rhythm quickened, she began to move in a dance that, while not consciously provocative, set the onlookers to breathing hard with the grip of its allure. Like the music instrument in itself, her body, slender and seductive, seemed to vibrate in a wild melody all its own.

As she danced, the shawl about the girls head came loose and was tossed aside, letting the glorious mass of her hair stream about her shoulders, enveloping them in a cascade of coppery gold. She was like a spinning torch, a veritable pillar of flame, and a roar of approval came from the audience. With an effort of will, Onesimus tore his eyes from the girl and studied Domitian. Naked lust was in the Roman's eyes, and Onesimus wondered if the girl had any conception of what her dancing could do to the souls of men, or of the danger that might come to her because of it.

Leah laughed exultantly in the midst of her dancing and, deliberately, provocative now, whirled before the tall tribune, eyes mocking him. Faster the rhythm went as she moved about the open circle in the crowd, skillfully eluding those who tried to touch her. Coins began to fall in a shower upon the stones as the music rose to its climax, then ceased upon a crash of the cymbals. Standing on her tip toes, her lovely young breasts rising and falling rapidly with the excitement and approval of her dancing. Leah of Petra poised like a statue of Aphrodite herself, eyes shining, cheeks bright with color, while the crowd deepened the spontaneous thunder of its applause.

Onesimus was the first to see the rich color drain suddenly from her cheeks, leaving them marble-pale. For an instant, she was rigid, as if truly transformed into a statue of the goddess of love, then she wavered and took a quick step as if to regain her balance. Sensing what was happening, he started toward her, darting between several men who stood between him and the open space where she stood. But he was too far away, and it was the tribune Domitian who caught the slender body of the dancer in his arms as she toppled over in a dead faint.

## 2

For a moment as the Roman officer lowered the unconscious girl to the ground, the crowd stood paralyzed. Then someone shouted, "Away! She is possessed by a demon!" Those in front began at once to push back, for everyone knew that demons sometimes left those who were possessed, particular during a period of unconsciousness, and enter the body of a well person. Only Onesimus moved toward the girl and the kneeling tribune.

"You there!" he barked at Onesimus. "Help me with this girl." Onesimus knelt beside the unconscious dancer. As he felt for the pulse of her wrist, her body began to jerk convulsively. A torrent of words poured from her throat. They seem to be a confused jumble of childhood phrases, then cries of protest, as if someone were punishing her, and finally screams of agony and a writhing of her body as if under the lash. The whole episode lasted only a moment, then as if the torrent of words had released some of the energy inside the slender body, she was quiet.

"Is it the sacred disease?" the tribune asked. Epilepsy, thought to result from possession by demons, was often called the "sacred disease," although Hippocrates had argued nearly five hundred years before it was no different from other diseases. She had not bitten her tongue, and there was no froth at her mouth, such as how Hippocrates had described in what he had preferred to call the "great disease."

"Answer me!" the tribune barked irritably. "It must be the sacred disease."

"I do not believe it is the sacred disease, but I'm not a physician," he told the Roman confidently.

"What then?" They did not realize that the girl had opened her eyes and was listening to them.

"A faint perhaps," Onesimus admitted, "from the dancing. Or she could be possessed."

Leah of Petra sat up quickly, her cheeks burning with indignation. "Am I deaf," she demanded angrily, "that you speak ill of me to my face?"

Onesimus smiled. "No one speaks ill of you. You were dancing and fainted. The noble tribune caught you and I offered to help."

The girl's anger seemed to depart as suddenly as it had come. She smiled, but upon the handsome Roman, not Onesimus in the dingy robe. "I regret if I have troubled you, noble sir," she said graciously in flawless Greek, and again Onesimus marveled at her self-possession and her manners. Most girls her age would have been dumb before the magnificence of the Roman tribune.

The tribune bowed with equal grace. "My name is Domitian." explained the tribune. "Words are inadequate to describe your beauty and talent. If you still feel faint, my uncle's villa is only a short distance away. A glass of wine would help. You can ride in my carriage."

But something else had claimed the girl's thoughts. "Hadja!" she called to the leader of the musicians, who waited nearby. "What of the coins? There should be many."

The Nabatean smiled and held out his cupped hands. They were almost filled with gold and silver. "We picked them up, O Living Flame, while you lay in the fit."

Leah stamped her foot. "How many times must I tell you I do not have fits?" she cried angrily.

"Then you have had them before?" Onesimus asked.

"Sometimes when I dance, I grow faint. It is nothing." She stood up but swayed, and Onesimus caught her or she would have fallen. Her body was soft under his fingers about her waist, and he could not deny the stirring of his pulses at the contact.

"Let me carry you to my uncle's villa to recover," Domitian suggested eagerly.

"I am all right now." The girl pushed away Onesimus's supporting hand. "Thank you for your kindness, sir," she said graciously to Domitian. "I must return to my house with my musicians."

"Then you must sing and dance at a banquet I'm giving at my villa next week. There will be several high officials of the Roman government present. You will not be alone. Others will also be there to entertain." Leah stiffened as he reached down and fondled a lock of her hair covering her breast, and then smiling, he continued. "Those who dance at my table are well rewarded. Can I count on you?"

Looking around at her musicians, and knowing that this was her chance to make a great deal of money, Leah excitedly inquired, "Can I bring my musicians?"

"I would rather you didn't. However, if that is your wish, then bring them," agreed Domitian reluctantly.

While this was going on, Aquila took Onesimus off to the side and whispered, "I know of this Domitian. He is the son of Vespasian who many contend will be emperor some day. I have heard stories of cruelty concerning Domitian. His fondness for the wine cup and women are well known."

Taking his leave, Domitian was flanked by two Roman soldiers, pushing the people aside to make way for the tribune. One of the soldiers shoved Timothy who fell beside Onesimus. Sudden rage gripped the heart of Onesimus. He who had always obeyed Roman law, found himself tired of the belligerent attitude of Roman military. Dropping his sack of belongings, Onesimus quickly stepped in front of the soldier who had pushed his new friend to the ground, and grabbing the soldier, he lifted him over his head and threw him into the other soldier and the tribune, knocking them to the ground. There was a groan of pain and a deafening silence from the crowd.

"Are you hurt, Timothy?" Onesimus asked, as he helped him up.

"No, I'm all right," he insisted, "but neither of us will be healthy if we stay here, come!" As they quickly turned to leave, one of the musicians signaled them to follow him. The crowd parted as they ran after the musician. Immediately Aquila and the other Christians moved to fill the gap creating a protective barrier, giving time for Onesimus and Timothy to escape.

Darkness was almost upon them as they ran down the narrow streets and passage ways. The musician finally led them into an opening in a building, down stone steps and into a large room, modestly furnished.

"You will be safe here for the night," the musician pointed out breathlessly. "I don't believe they will search for you. There are too many places to hide. I guess I should introduce myself. I am called Hadja."

"I am Onesimus, and this is Timothy," Onesimus explained. "It is kind of you to let us stay in your house tonight. Thank you for your help. I hope we don't get you in trouble."

"Don't worry about it," Hadja replied. "You did what I've wanted to do for months. We sailed from Caesarea last fall with the hope of making a fortune from the Romans."

Onesimus broke in, "Isn't it dangerous for her to sing and dance in the streets?"

"Of course, there is always danger everywhere, but we are always with her," Hadja answered reassuringly.

"I have never heard a more lovely voice, nor have I seen a more graceful dancer," insisted Onesimus.

"Few can equal the Living Flame, although she is only eighteen. As a dancer and singer in the great cities of the empire,

I am sure she could turn the heads of kings if she wished. This is the reason she accepted the invitation to sing and dance at the tribune's banquet. There will be many fat purses at the banquet, and the prospect of many more engagements to come. It is the break she has been hoping for."

The sound of footsteps interrupted their conversation. It was Leah and the other musicians.

"Leah, this is Onesimus and Timothy," Hadja said.

"That was a stupid thing you did, Onesimus," Leah stated. "You are lucky you and your friend are still alive." Turning to Hadja, she asked, "The Roman who caught me, I acted as if I knew him and where his villa is but, I didn't."

"He is Domitian, son of Vespasian."

Leah stiffened for a moment, then relaxed as she replied, "He is very handsome. Is it true that his father has slave girls from the east who dance naked before him?"

Timothy blushed, "A young girl should not even think such things," he scolded.

"Don't tell me what to think, I am eighteen and I do as I please," she said sharply, "but you two should be very careful where you go. The praetorian guard may be looking for you." Leah looked at Onesimus and smiled. Her entire manner changed in one of those transformations which Onesimus had witnessed back on the street where she danced. "Perhaps I was wrong about you."

"What do you mean?" inquired Onesimus.

"Well, after seeing how big and strong you are, maybe I should pray for the Roman tribune instead of you." Onesimus could not help but laugh. "Have you two been in Rome long?" she asked.

"We have just arrived," replied Timothy. Onesimus and I met on the road into the capital city. I have just graduated from the school of Tyrannius in Ephesus, and I'm here on a mission."

"Tyrannius?" inquired Leah excitedly.

"Yes," replied Timothy, "do you know him?"

Leah looked soberly at Timothy and asked, "Are you a Christian?"

There was a pause as Timothy looked around at the others. The room was suddenly quiet. "Yes, I am a Christian. I have come at the request of Paul the Apostle. He asked me to bring his cloak and his scrolls."

"You are a brave man, Timothy," she said with a sigh, "but don't go around Rome telling people that you are a Christian. It could mean your head. Nero is a mad man, and he is having many Christians killed for no apparent reason, so be very careful."

"I felt that I could trust you, or I would not have revealed my identity," Timothy admitted.

"I too am a Christian," Leah stated, "but my faith has been extremely weak since coming to Rome. I'm afraid Paul has been disappointed in me recently. I live only to accomplish a goal that I have set for myself." Leah tossed her head and turned to leave. "I must go to the market and buy supper for Demetrius."

"Demetrius? Who is he?" Onesimus inquired.

"The maker of lyres. He lives on the street of the Greeks, and I live with him," she added matter of factly.

Onesimus was shocked by her casual admission that she lived with a man. "Demetrius is a lucky man to have such a beautiful woman who can sing and dance as you can," he added.

Leah smiled at the compliment. "Demetrius has taught me since I was twelve years old. I owe him my life." Then she added, "If you plan to see Paul tomorrow, Hadja will give you directions to his house."

As Leah was leaving, Onesimus expressed his concern for her. "Please don't go to Domitian's banquet," he begged.

"I must," she answered firmly. "Please do not worry about me. I do hope we shall see each other again."

"We will," Onesimus promised. "We will."

Hadja set out fruit and wine for his guests. After visiting for a while, Onesimus and Timothy rolled out their pallets for the night.

It seemed to Onesimus as he lay trying to sleep that he must be bewitched. Or, he thought, one of the demons said to possess the girl might have escaped from her body into his. Whatever the cause, he could not get her out of his mind, and even in his dreams, he kept hearing her voice and seeing her body spinning like a torch in the dance. But just when he was going to take her in his arms, she was snatched away by a Roman tribune named Domitian.

# 3

Onesimus and Timothy made their way down the Sacra Via, the street leading to the center of imperial government of Rome. The market place was crowded with people from all walks of life. On the narrow colonnaded streets that led each way from the market place, they noticed tall Macedonians as they jostled along. Soldiers from Gaul, Egyptians, Cypriots, Phoenicians, Jews, Persians, and occasionally a slant-eyed citizen of the empire far to the east walked the stone-paved streets. There were hawkers in small stalls shouting their wares. In the babble of voices, only one language was common, the everyday Greek that nearly everybody spoke with one accent or another.

The hour was too early for the courtesans, who rarely showed their faces and as much of their bodies as they dared before darkness, but men were everywhere. Ruddy faces on their way home from the baths, where they spent most of the day. A white-robed prince of the desert tribes that lived in the land beyond the Red Sea, walked proudly through the crowd, until pushed aside roughly by a Roman officer in magnificently polished harness, followed by two soldiers with drawn swords, in case their leader became suddenly involved in a fight that often broke out among so many nationalities jammed together like this.

"Quick," whispered Timothy, grabbing Onesimus by the arm and pushing themselves into the crowd. "It could be Domitian,"

"No, it's not Domitian," Onesimus assured Timothy. "I would know that guy anywhere. But I agree we must be careful."

Near the market place were many open-fronted eating places, where attendants had already begun setting out food samples. Preserved figs and dates, gourds of wine, smoked fish, all were temptingly displayed before the chattering crowd.

The voices of women shrieked back and forth across the narrow streets which led from the market area, laughing, shouting obscene jokes, singing, or calling out a frank invitation to men passing on the street below.

"I have seen much of the same kind of traffic in Ephesus but not with such intensity, boldness, and carelessness," Timothy said gravely.

Following the directions Hadja gave them, they came to Paul's rented house. They were warmly greeted. Mark, having spent the night at Aquila and Priscilla's house, was already there. Paul was delighted to have his scrolls and cloak that Timothy brought at his request. Onesimus felt an immediate bond with this bald-headed aging man.

Paul remembered vividly the first day he arrived in Rome, some eighteen months ago. He was consigned to a filthy prison cell on the first day, but the next day, he was brought before Gallinus, one of the magistrates of the Imperial Court. Beside the magistrate, only a scribe with a pen, tablets, and parchment sheets sat at the table.

"You are Paul of Tarsus, remanded to Rome in the custody of centurion Julius by Festus, Procurator of Judea and Samaria, for trial before Caesar?" the magistrate asked.

"Yes, sir."

"Procurator Festus notes that you could have been set free, if you had not appealed to the Imperial Court. Why did you make such an appeal?"

"I was asked to return to Jerusalem and be tried before the Sanhedrin. But word came to me of Jews lying in wait to murder me before my trial."

"Good reason, no doubt." Gallinus smiled and said, "I served in Judea for five years. You Jews are a strange people, much given to killing each other over small differences of opinion." Then he picked up a scroll that lay on the table before the scribe and glanced at it briefly, then put it down. "You shall get nothing but justice from me. Until your accusers appear, you may live outside the prison, provided you are able to pay the rent of a house and the wages and food of the two soldiers who will guard you."

"I have been assured that friends of the prisoner will be glad to make such an arrangement," Julius broke in. "They are dependable people, known to me, and will make bond for him."

"Let it be so ordered," said Gallinus. "The prisoner, Paul of Tarsus, will remain in custodia militaris until such a time as his accusers appear."

"I have you to thank for this," he told Julius. "How can I ever repay you?"

"You have already repaid me by saving the entire crew when our ship was wrecked at Melita. All I did was ask Gallinus to give you a hearing and determine whether your case justified custodia militaris, instead of custodia publica. Your physician friend tells me you're subject to fevers, and I'm afraid the common jail wouldn't be a very healthy place for you."

"But the hire of the soldiers? And the rent of a house?"

"Thank Luke and your friends, Aquila and Priscilla, for that."

"Luke left everything behind at Troas, when he chose to go with me. He certainly couldn't afford to pay for all that."

"You forget that he once served as a surgeon to the legions at Antioch-in-Pisidia," said Julius. "In Rome, most doctors cater to the rich, and the soldiers of the Praetorian Guards have to make out as best they can. They were fortunate and happy to employ a physician of Luke's skill."

"If I'm to dwell nearby, I had better find a home for myself and my guards," said Paul.

"Aquila took care of that," Julius assured him. "I sent a soldier ahead. When we get there, your chains can be transferred to him."

The house, Paul discovered, was ample for the needs of him and his friends and his two guards, one by day and one by night. Aquila and Priscilla were already waiting for him and a happy reunion followed, tempered only by Paul's feeling of guilt at being forced to accept charity even from old friends.

The chatter and laughter of Paul's friends brought his mind back to the present. "Timothy, tell me about our church in Ephesus."

"The church is doing quite well. I have just graduated from the School of Tyrannus, and ready to pastor a church," explained Timothy.

"Wonderful, my son, but stay here with me for awhile. Since Mark is staying at Aquila's house, there is room here for you and your friend Onesimus."

Late that afternoon, Luke came home from his appointments. He a man small in stature and pushing sixty, but highly respected as a physician and personal care giver to Paul. He was delighted to see Timothy and Mark and was extremely impressed with Onesimus. "God has given you a magnificent physical body," Luke stated as he looked at Onesimus. "It has been given to you for a purpose. And God will reveal it to you in His own time."

"Thank you," replied Onesimus. "I have often wondered why I am so much taller than the average man. I suppose standing head and shoulders above most, gives me an advantage."

"Yes," agreed Luke. "Aquila tells me you had a run-in with Domitian."

"I apologize for my anger," stated Onesimus. "But I didn't like that my friend Timothy was pushed to the ground."

"You must be careful and watch where you go for the next few days. Perhaps the incident will be forgotten soon."

"I have run out of funds and am anxious to find work. Do you know where I might find employment?" asked Onesimus.

"Nero has begun to build a huge colosseum for the entertainment of the populace. However, most all the labor is furnished by slaves," Luke informed him. "If I were you, I think I would pass on that. But I have something you might consider. My patient load is quite heavy, especially at the praetorium. Would you consider being my assistant? If you are interested and willing to learn, I could teach you many things about medicine."

"Yes! Yes, I would love to help you. Thank you," replied Onesimus excitedly.

"I can't pay you much, but enough to take care of your needs, plus room and board."

Their conversations went well into the night, and Onesimus found it hard to go to sleep. He was thinking about his new opportunity and the conversation of slave labor at the colosseum brought back his feeling of guilt about leaving Philemon. But his last thought before sleep came was of a beautiful woman with flaming red hair named Leah of Petra.

4

When Onesimus woke up the next morning, he heard laughter coming from the main room. Priscilla had brought
breakfast for everyone. Onesimus was hungry, and thanked
Priscilla for the food.

Paul was heartened by the coming of Timothy from Galatia
and the arrival of Mark from Asia. There was also Aristarchus, a
fellow prisoner from Judea, Silas, who had accompanied Paul on
his second missionary journey and Demas, a Greek convert. Luke,
of course, had come with Paul from Caesarea, and now Onesimus.

Altogether, it was a busy household there in the shadow of
the praetorium, with delegations of Christians who had come
to Rome to visit the apostle being received daily and letters
written to churches throughout the empire. Nor did Paul give up
his attempt to bring the Jews of Rome to a realization that the
expected Messiah had come and that salvation for them, as for
everyone, was now possible.

The Jewish colony in Rome was a large one, having been
established centuries before, when Pompey had brought many
of them to Rome as slaves after his successful campaigns in the
east. Prized for their intelligence and their willingness to work

ceaselessly for their own freedom and advancement, Jewish slaves had always been in great demand, so a considerable body of them, as well as freedmen, had grown up in Rome.

Preserving the old customs and still loyal to the temple at Jerusalem, they exerted a considerable influence on the business affairs of Rome and a section of the city had been adopted by them as their residence. Called the Trastevere, it lay across the river from the imperial palace. And since this area was easily reached by way of bridges crossing the river from the central part of the city, Paul was able to spend considerable time there, attempting to show the Jews, too, the way of salvation.

Like many cities, Rome had found the burial of the dead a major problem, especially with the slaughter of so many Christians. Lest it become entirely surrounded by cemeteries and literally be squeezed to death by the presence of its own dead, the authorities had ordered tombs excavated from the soft volcanic earth in this area. Thus there had come into being a city of the dead beneath the ground, known as the catacombs, with galleries, rooms, and tunnels with niches on each side carved in the soft rock for the dead.

Luke's first appointment of the day was a request that he wait upon Demetrius, the lyre maker. Onesimus, curious about the man Leah admitted living with and, excited about the prospect of seeing her again. He watched Luke bustling about, dipping a fresh supply of lean and slender leeches from the tank where he kept them, and renewing his supply of medicine.

The home of the lyre maker was fairly large, although not pretentious. Most of the Greeks on this street were artisans, silversmiths, or tailors, and lived well, but the sounds that poured from the house of Demetrius were foreign to such occupations. From the back came the uncertain sound of a lyre, as if a student were practicing, and behind the musical sounds was the steady tapping of hammers on wood as workmen put together resonant frames and sounding boards upon which strings were stretched.

Leah was nowhere to be seen when the Nabatean escorted Luke and Onesimus through the house into the garden. It was a typical Roman house, with an open court, or atrium, in the center of which water from a pipe poured into a shallow pool. It was easy to believe that Leah of Petra lived here, for the flowers were gay with color, like herself.

"Come over here, Luke." The speaker was a plump Greek in his sixties, sitting on a bench. He held a cithara which he had apparently been tuning, for a delicately carved set of ivory pipes lay on the bench beside him. The Greeks eyes were deep-set in his round face and lit with amusement, as if the owner saw only merriment in the world. Onesimus felt an instinctive liking for the fat man, in spite of his soiled robe and the aromatic smell of wine that he exuded.

"Thank you for coming, Luke. My gout is giving me problems," he stated as he observed Onesimus. "I am Demetrius, young man."

"But Leah said she lived with—" Onesimus stopped, crimson with embarrassment.

"Is there anything wrong with her living with me," Demetrius asked.

"Of course not," Onesimus said. "I was a fool."

"No more than almost anyone would have been under the circumstances," the Greek replied. "When a beautiful girl says she lives with a man, you naturally think the worst. Look at me young man. Do I look like a debaucher of young women?" Demetrius suddenly began laughing, holding his vast belly as if he were afraid it would come apart with its shaking. Finally he stopped laughing and wiped his streaming eyes with his sleeve. "Alas," he added with mock sadness, "even if I longed for feminine solace, who would love a fat old man for anything but his money, of which I have next to none, anyway?"

"I did not mean that there was anything wrong in her living with you," Onesimus assured him sincerely.

"Of course you didn't. But you must have heard other people insinuate things about her that are not true. Women envy Leah for her beauty because men are drawn to her in the street. And the men, realizing how pale and insipid their own wives are beside her, label her a meretrix so they will not feel so guilty about lusting after her."

"You are a philosopher," Onesimus exclaimed admiringly.

"Nay, I am but a wine bibber who has known many people, most of them bad. Because I acknowledge no god who would forbid me, I do as I please, but I harm no one except myself, which is my privilege. Since I like to see people happy and gay, I let Leah sing and dance that others might share her beauty and her talent. But sit down beside me, young man, and let Luke look at my leg. Leah has gone to sell a lyre for me and bring back a fish for our dinner. Luke, what do you think of the spell she had the other day?"

"I do not believe it is the sacred disease," replied Luke.

"Nor I. What do you really think of these fits of hers," he asked.

"I have seen them in young girls before," Luke said. "But most of them grew out of it with womanhood."

"Leah told me you were there young man. Did she say anything when she was in the fit?"

"Only the babbling of a child. She seemed to be remembering a scene where someone was beating her."

"I was hoping she had forgotten all that," Demetrius sighed. "I took Leah when she was twelve years old. Her father was a trapper of doves and a petty thief. He had beaten her several times and was on the point of selling her to a Roman, but I gave him a higher price. I adopted her legally and taught her all I knew of music, philosophy, and the arts. Now the lyre is not so popular and I have been working to improve the cithara, so we have not fared so well. Leah loves to sing and dance, so since people will pay to hear her, I let her perform sometimes in the streets."

"Is it safe?" asked Onesimus.

"The Nabateans are always there. And Hadja would give his life for her."

"You trained her well," Onesimus said. "I never heard a more lovely voice, nor saw a more graceful dancer."

Demetrius nodded, "Few can equal her, although she is still little more than a child. I'm sure she could turn the heads of kings if she wished. But I place her happiness above everything else and so I hesitate to take her away from Rome."

The first thought Onesimus had was that Leah would be better off away from cities that were so wicked and sinful, perhaps married to a good and serious young man who would love her and provide her wants and make her happy. Such a man, he thought with quickening pulse, as he. But his own ambition had sensed a kindred spirit within Leah of Petra. "I doubt if Leah will be truly happy until she has done the things upon which her heart is set."

"You have a wise head upon your shoulders," Demetrius said approvingly. "I have been trying to avoid the same conclusion for many months. But since we have no money for traveling, we must stay here, for the time being at least.

From a jar, Luke took a leech and placed it upon Demetrius's swollen leg. Then from his pouch, he measured out a dose of poppy leaves and mixed them with wine. Demetrius drank the mixture with a grimace. "Give it a few minutes and the pain should subside."

He picked up the cithara from the bench beside him. "Listen closely to the tones of this instrument." When he touched the strings, the air throbbed with a melody.

Onesimus recognized the touch of a master, even though the fingers of the lyre maker were pudgy and short. Leah had learned her lessons well, he thought, for she, too, possessed the same loving touch upon the strings. "I am no musician," he confessed. "But the tones have a fullness and a resonance I never heard before."

"Exactly. And do you know why?"

"No, I know nothing of music."

"Plato warned against trying to separate the soul from the body," Demetrius told him. "Music is food for the soul, and when the soul is healthy, so usually is the body."

"I have noticed how grief and sadness can bring sickness," Onesimus admitted. "Some believe that the same demons—"

"Demons, bah!" Demetrius spat eloquently into the grass at his feet. "The demons that possess man are born within himself, children of his own desires. Me, I drink too much wine when I can get it, which isn't often. And I eat too much when I can afford it, which is practically never. But I am happy, and so this blubber-fat body of mine runs as smoothly as a water clock." He laid down the instrument. "But I weary you two with this talk of music. It's one of the penalties of growing old."

"We have other patients to see," Luke said, "so we must be on our way. I will have Onesimus stop by tomorrow and see how you are doing."

"I shall be here, and thank you for coming by."

# 5

O nesimus stopped at the doorway leading to the garden of Demetrius when he came the next morning for a follow-up visit with Luke's patient, unwilling to interrupt the beautiful and peaceful scene before him by making his presence known. Demetrius was sitting on a bench and Leah sat on the grass at his feet, with the morning sunlight turning her unbound hair into a coppery cascade. She touched the lyre in her hands with skilled fingers, and her voice filled the garden.

"Beautiful!" Onesimus cried from the doorway, unable to remain silent. Leah jumped to her feet. "Onesimus," she cried. "What do you mean creeping up on us?"

"The song was too beautiful to interrupt," Onesimus explained.

"He is right, Leah." Demetrius smiled fondly at her. "It was a lucky day when I found you weeping in the streets of Capernaum."

The girls face sobered. "But mainly for me. I was twelve years old, Onesimus, but already I had known what it was to be beaten without reason and to be stripped naked for men to set a price upon me. Demetrius was the first person who had ever been kind to me in my whole life," she added. "Do you wonder that I love him more than anyone else in the world?"

Onesimus bent to examine the legs of Demetrius. He found that the swelling had already subsided noticeably.

"Truly," Demetrius said, "if anyone had told me yesterday there would be so little pain today, I would have branded him a liar."

"Not all physicians would have treated you so well as Luke did," Leah stated. "And now Onesimus is learning from him. Most people say Luke is the best physician in Rome."

"How do you know so much?" Onesimus asked with a smile.

"I go everywhere and keep my eyes open." Leah tossed her head. "Besides, men have no secrets from a woman."

"So you call yourself a woman now. Soon you will be eyeing young men, and then there will be no more singing in the house of Demetrius."

Leah ran to him and put her smooth cheek against his grizzled one. "You know I would never leave you," she cried, and Onesimus was amazed to see tears in her eyes, so quickly had her volatile emotions changed.

Demetrius squeezed her shoulder. "I was only jesting," he soothed. "Someday you will marry a rich man who will make old Demetrius the keeper of his wine cellar. Then I can die happy."

Onesimus could stay no longer, but as he went about the city visiting the sick that he and Luke saw the day before, his thoughts were full of Leah's gaiety, her beauty, and the way her mood could change from happy to sad and back again in an instant, like a child. He had seen no signs of prosperity in the house of Demetrius, but he found there something more important, a quality often lacking in the homes of the rich. The happiness of people who loved unreservedly.

When Onesimus arrived home that evening, he was greeted by the fragrant aroma of fish broiling on the coals of the cooking hearth. Luke who had come home earlier, greeted him, as did Paul. And when he went into the kitchen, he saw Priscilla at the hearth, who had come to prepare the evening meal for Paul's household. She was not alone. Leah was sitting on a low stool, watching the preparation for the evening meal and chattering all the while.

"Welcome to our house, Leah of Petra."

Leah's eyes twinkled. "I am part Greek and bear a gift."

"Look at the fine fish Leah brought us," Priscilla said proudly. "I have persuaded her to stay and help eat it."

"Will you dance for us afterward?" Onesimus asked.

Leah held up her hands in mock horror. "Do you want your neighbors to say you are entertaining a Jezebel?"

While Priscilla prepared supper, Luke took Leah and Onesimus into his small surgical room where he treated the poor of the city. It was little more than a covered terrace with a closet for his medicines and instruments.

Leah listened with interest while Luke demonstrated the instruments and their uses. The bag he carried on his rounds was called the Nartik. It contained the izmel, or scalpel, for incising abscesses; the trephine, a nail for letting blood; the makdeijach, a sharp pointed probe with which to explore wounds; the misporayim, a pair of scissors for cutting dressings or the sutures of horsehair sometimes used to close wounds; and the kalbo, a pair of forceps which had many uses.

On another shelf was the kulcha, for emptying the stomach in poisonings; the gubtha, a hollow catheter for cases of urinary stone or obstruction.

In the closet that served as a pharmacy and treatment room were the drugs; borit, a strong soap for washing inflamed skin, as well as the hands of the physician; tsri, the healing balm; and lott, a powerful sedative made from opium. Next to them were various ointments.

Below these another shelf was filled with jars of powdered poppy leaves for promoting sleep and relieving pain. At the end of the shelf was a pile of odd-looking roots. Onesimus picked one up and handed it to Leah.

"Why it looks like a man," she explained. "See? Here are the arms, and the legs, and body. What is it?"

"The root is called 'mandragora.'" Luke took down a bottle filled with dark fluid. "This is the wine of mandragora, made by soaking the powdered root in wine to extract the active drug. But the wine of mandragora is mainly used for relieving pain and in nervous afflictions.

"When the drug is used to cause sleep," she asked, "do they ever wake up again?"

"Not always, but a very large dose is required to cause death."

Leah shivered. "You said mandragora was used for nervous afflictions. I only faint when I am excited. Would it help to prevent the attacks?"

"It should," Luke agreed. "Let me give you a small bottle of mandragora wine to take home tonight. You can try a few doses when you are going to dance. It might keep off the attacks altogether."

The fish was perfectly cooked and the meal was gay, for Leah was as intelligent and witty as she was beautiful. Much of the time, Onesimus forgot to eat for looking at her. Afterward he walked with her across the city to the street of the Greeks. "I love Priscilla, Onesimus," she told him as they stood before her house. "And you are very sweet too." She stood on tiptoe and kissed him on the cheek, then she was gone.

Priscilla did not miss the warm light in his eyes when he returned, still a little dazed by that feathery kiss.

"Leah is very beautiful, Onesimus," she observed. "And she likes you very much."

"But she sings and dances in the streets," he reminded her with mock disapproval.

"Did not David the King sing and dance in honor of the Most High?" she stated.

"Some call her a Jezebel and accuse her of being a prostitute."

"Some women envy all girls with beauty and speak evil of them," Priscilla said with a sniff. "Leah has spirit and would make a fine wife for a bright young man. She likes you, Onesimus. You should court her." Onesimus blushed and did not argue the point.

Along with assisting Luke, Paul was also using Onesimus in running errands and assisting him whenever he needed help. The morning after his conversation with Priscilla, Onesimus was on an errand for Paul when he decided to go by the house of Demetrius hoping to see Leah.

Leah came out of the house carrying a lyre. "Good morning, Onesimus," greeting him with a smile.

"Good morning to you," he replied. "I am running an errand for the Apostle Paul. Where are you going?"

"I am delivering this to the street of the dove sellers," she said. "May I walk with you?"

"I am glad Demetrius is doing better, but then I will have no more excuse to visit his house."

"But you can come to see us anytime you wish."

"If I come without being called, people will say I am paying court to you."

"No one has ever paid court to me, Onesimus," she said softly, and then her voice grew bitter. "The young men are afraid because their mothers call me a Jezebel. Why is it a sin to want to be happy?" she demanded.

"Priscilla does not think you are a Jezebel."

"I know." She put her hand on his, and her fingers were warm and very much alive as the curled around about his own. "She is sweet like you, Onesimus, and I love her."

"Priscilla thinks I should marry, and she has already picked out the girl."

Leah did not look at him, but he saw her lips soften in a smile.

"She is a very lovely girl named Leah of Petra," he added.

"Don't you have anything to say about the matter?" she asked as her eyes twinkled.

They were crossing a small park and at the moment were screened from view by a clump of trees. Onesimus pulled her around to face him. "You know I love you very much, Leah," he said.

"But you don't know me at all, Onesimus. I am vain and forgetful."

"And very beautiful…"

"Greedy and thoughtless…"

"And loveable…"

She stamped her foot in mock anger. "Will you let me finish? I am telling you that I am not the kind of wife you deserve. I would embarrass you, and people would talk about me."

"What would all that matter when we loved each other?" He drew her close. "It is that you don't love me, Leah?"

"Oh, I do love you, Onesimus," she said then in a rush, "I do, I do. But I love Demetrius, too, and he comes first."

"Demetrius himself told me he thought you might be happier married to the right man."

"He was only trying to protect me." Suddenly she clung to him and he held her there, asking nothing more, content to savor the sweetness of having her in his arms. When she lifted her face from his breast, he kissed her and found the sweetness of her mouth mixed with the salt of her tears. Finally she pushed him away and wiped her tears upon the sleeve of his robe. "We must be sensible, Onesimus," she said firmly. "I can't possibly marry you. Not for a long time."

"But why?"

"It's a long story, but you deserve to hear it. Years ago, Demetrius was the director of the Alexandrian Theater and the most famous musician in the empire. He loved a girl named Althea and trained her to be the leading actress there. She was his mistress and he adored her, so he could not believe she would be untrue to him. But she took up with a rich Roman and tried to get rid of Demetrius by telling her lover that he was a leader in a plot against the Romans.

Demetrius barely escaped with his life and a little money by joining a caravan going to Demascus, but some thieves robbed him in Capernaum and left him for dead near the lake. Simon Peter found him and nursed him back to health. From what Simon told me, he was about to kill himself when I came to him. Since then, I have been his whole life. Demetrius set up shop for making lyres, and from the sale of lyres and my dancing in the streets of Capernaum, we saved enough money to book passage on a ship to Rome. He taught me everything I know, Onesimus, and he lives only for the time when he can make me the most famous singer and dancer in the empire. It will be his revenge upon Althea."

"But Demetrius loves you enough to want your happiness, Leah."

"Don't you see?" she pleaded. "I have to do this for Demetrius. He says I am more talented than Althea was and that I will only need to sing and dance before royalty to be accepted immediately." Remembering the living flame of her body when he had seen her dancing in the street, Onesimus could understand the confidence of the lyre maker.

"This new cithara Demetrius had made is far superior to the old ones," Leah continued. "It is bound to be in great demand in a city the size of Rome. We can live on what he makes from selling the cithara if we have to, but I would sing and dance in the streets to make him happy. No one but me can ever realize how much I owe him, Onesimus."

Loving her as he did, Onesimus could not find it in his heart to try to dissuade her. He understood the inner fire of ambition that burned within her.

"This banquet that Domitian spoke of several days ago, has he sent word to you as to when it might be?"

"Not as yet."

"I hope you deny his request. You are a beautiful girl, and I saw the way he looked at you."

"Men look at me every day. Do you think I can't read what is in their eyes?" She wrinkled her nose at him. "The tribune is a very handsome man and free with his gold. He gave Hadja twenty denarii."

"But you know how these Romans are. A young girl is not safe—"

"Onesimus!" she cried delightedly. "You are jealous!"

"Of course I'm jealous," he admitted. "Didn't I just finish telling you I love you and want to marry you? But just the same, the Romans are evil and not to be trusted."

Her face sobered, "I know all about Romans; my father was going to sell me to one of them. But they pay well and we need their gold. Besides, I never dance without Hadja and his men, and any one of them could kill a man with his bare hands. Don't worry, my love, I will be safe even in Domitian's villa."

# PART II

# THE EVIL TRIBUNE

# 6

Leah was in her garden the next day when the messenger from Domitian was ushered in. She had been learning a new song, and she put down the lyre as the visitor bowed before her. He was tall and imposing in appearance.

"I am the nomenclator of Domitian," the man said loftily. "Where is she who is called Leah of Petra?"

Leah's heart jumped. "I am Leah of Petra," she said.

"Domitian bids you attend a banquet to be given at his villa on the river Tiber this evening, to sing and dance for his guests."

"Are you sure he wants me?" she asked.

"Quite sure."

The thrill of being summoned to the tribune's palace swept from her mind all memory of Onesimus's warning and the unsavory things she had heard about the orgies held in the Roman villas. She thought only that here was a chance to earn a large sum of money.

"Will you come?" the slave asked politely, although his manner said it was unthinkable that anyone should refuse the summons of such a high-ranking officer.

Leah had recovered her poise now. "You may tell your master that I shall be honored to dance before him and his guests this evening," she said with considerable dignity. "My musicians and I will be there at dusk."

The nomenclator's eyebrows rose. "The banquet has its own musicians."

Now Leah remembered Onesimus's warning. "I dance to no music save that played by my own troupe," she said firmly. "They accompany me wherever I go."

The slave shrugged. "Bring them then. Perhaps Domitian forgot to mention them."

As the slave was turning away, she said quickly, "Could you tell me what my pay will be?"

"Entertainers do not demand pay for pleasing the son of Vespasian," the nomenclator explained. "It is enough to say they received a summons to appear before him." But seeing the disappointment in her face, he added kindly, "It is customary, however, to throw a purse to those he likes."

"A purse? How large?"

"No sum is set. A thousand sesterces, perhaps, if you prove particularly agreeable to him."

"A thousand sesterces!" Leah gasped, but quickly recovered her composure. "Of course I shall be honored to dance for your master, whatever the purse," she said graciously.

The nomenclator bowed again, as if he were enjoying this little farce. "Can you direct me to the house of the leech, Luke of Troas, here in Rome," he asked.

"What has Luke done?" Leah asked quickly.

"Domitian's mother who is staying at his villa while her husband Vespasian is in Israel would have the services of the leech."

Quickly Leah gave the directions to Luke's home. "If you see him," she added, "please don't tell him I'm dancing tonight." She blushed. "I have a reason for the request."

When the slave was gone, Leah rushed to the room where Demetrius was bedded with a cold, solaced no little by a bottle of wine she had bought that morning. "Demetrius!" she cried excitedly. "Demetrius! The most wonderful thing has happened!"

Leah threw her arms around his neck. "Would a thousand sesterces make you feel better?"

Demetrius was accustomed to her bursts of enthusiasm.

"A thousand sesterces is quite a bit if we had them."

"Oh, but we do have them! Or we will, after tonight."

"What do you mean?"

"I am to dance for Domitian and some high-ranking officers of the government tonight."

Demetrius sat up in bed, clutching the wine bottle. "Where did you get this crazy idea, child?"

"It's not crazy!" she stamped her foot. "Domitian's nomenclator was here just now and ask me to dance at a dinner tonight. And he mentioned a purse of a thousand sesterces if I entertain Domitian and his guests well."

"A thousand sesterces," Demetrius repeated and fell back on the bed. "I have not seen that much money since I was in Alexandria some years ago. Let me see: If Domitian likes you, other rich Romans who have villas on the river will want you to dance for them." Then his face grew serious. "But is it safe for you to go to his villa?"

"You and Onesimus are old women!" Leah cried in disgust. "I am not a child any longer, Demetrius, and besides, Hadja and the others will be there to guard me." She dropped to her knees beside the bed and tears came to her eyes. "You must let me go," she pleaded. "It will mean so much to us all."

"We do need the money badly," Demetrius admitted, smoothing the rich waves of her hair with pudgy fingers. "But promise me that you will keep Hadja and his men with you always."

"I promise." Leah leaped to her feet. "Now what will I wear? I know, the white stola of silk you gave me for my eighteenth birthday. And the palla over it, the yellow one. I was saving them to wear to something special. And Hadja must rent a cart and a mule for me to ride in, so I will not be too tired to dance well. And my hair! Oh, I have a thousand things to do." She was gone in a flurry of skirts.

It was dusk when Leah and her party arrived at the villa of Domitian and tied the mule and cart to a tree in the grove near the river. Leah had carried the package containing her silken stola and the yellow palla, plus fragile sandals of leather chased with a thin tracery of gold. A wall nearly ten feet high surrounded the elaborate palace. Most of the villas on the river had such high walls with steps running down to the water itself.

An armed guard let them through the gate, and the nomenclator met them in the atrium, as the central room of the house was called. Even in the darkness, they could see something of the beauty of the terraced gardens descending to the hillside to the water's edge and the fragrance of flowers was everywhere. Slaves in white garments moved about through the open terraces, carrying dishes to and from the triclinium, the banqueting room, where the dinner was already in progress.

The nomenclator raised his eyebrows at Leah's rough dress. "Is that your costume for dancing?" he asked, then a knowing smile came over his face. This girl was smart indeed, he thought, in choosing to dance naked before the revelers. Her slim loveliness would be a welcome change from the girls who usually entertain Domitian and his guests. Leah held up the package she carried. "I have my dress here for dancing," she explained. "Is there somewhere that I can change?"

"The entertainers dress for the performance in a room off the banqueting hall," the slave explained. "I will take you to it and show your musicians to the alcove where they will play." Through heavily curtained doorways on one side of the hall along which he took them came the sound of voices and laughter, the soft strains of the lyre and cithara, and the clink of glassware and cutlery. This was obviously the triclinium, and Leah judged that the doors across the corridor gave access to bedchambers.

The room to which she was ushered was a small but tastefully arranged, with a door to one side giving access to the triclinium. An elaborate dressing table occupied one wall, complete with perfume and cosmetics, antimony to whiten the cheeks, kohl for the eyelashes, henna for toes and fingernails, and everything that a beauty would use in her boudoir. In an open recess hung a rack of costumes, some of them so skimpy that they seemed not to exist at all. She had heard rumors that women danced in such costumes at the banquets of the Romans, while some were said to wear nothing at all. Now her startled eyes were seeing very evidence that the tales were true.

Leah had not admitted to Demetrius or to herself that she felt any apprehension about dancing before Domitian and his guests. But now that she was alone, with the shouts of the drunken revelers coming from the next room, she could not swallow the lump that insisted upon rising in her throat.

Quickly, before her courage could desert her, she took off her dress and underclothes and hung them over a chair. In a sudden burst of exuberance, she stretched her body luxuriously and whirled in a lithe dancing turn. Suddenly, though, she gave a little gasp and stooped quickly to hold her dress in front of her body. Only then did she realize that the lovely nude girl facing her on the other side of the room was her own reflection.

Timidly she crossed the room and touched the large mirror set into the wall, for she had never seen such a thing. Her whole body was reflected in it, the slender column of her head and neck, the lovely sloping lines of the shoulders merging with the taut fullness of small breasts, just now beginning to fill out with the promise of glorious womanhood, the sweet curves of a slender waist. No blemish showed anywhere in the perfect symmetry that faced her, and as she loosened her hair and let it fall upon her shoulders, the whole white length of her body seemed to take fire from it and glow with a warmth of its own.

Reluctantly Leah turned from the adoration of her own beauty to open the package she had brought. She wished now that she owned a length of silken cloth to wrap about her loins for an undergarment. Such as women were said to wear in Rome and the other rich cities of the empire. But silk was expensive, and so she could only draw on the thin knit trunks worn by ordinary people, when they wore any undergarment at all. Over the trunks went a linen undershirt and then the silken stola, a sleeveless dress cut along classical lines and girt just beneath the breasts with a band of silver ribbon.

Some women wore broad girdles of woven metal mesh, or fine leather chased with a filigree of gold or silver design, but Leah's slenderness needed no such disguise. The clinging fabric of the stola caressed her bosom lovingly and fell in straight silken folds from her waist to her ankles. Over the stola went the palla, a mantle usually worn out of doors, which she would drop as she poised to begin her dance.

There remained only to buckle on the light sandals, tying the thongs about her slender ankles, and she was ready. She scorned the cosmetics with which even young girls had begun to paint their faces, for her virginal loveliness needed no such artifice. Picking up an ivory brush from the table, she brushed her hair until it shone like molten copper. Next she tied over her hair a white silken shawl that she planned to wear while dancing.

Suddenly the door from the corridor opened and a girl came into the room. At the site of Leah, she stopped short and frowned. "Who are you?" she demanded abruptly.

The girl was older and her figure more generously curved, but it was her costume that startled Leah, for she wore a loose robe wrapped around her body. Beneath this revealing garment, the visitor seemed to be wearing only a small girdle of gold held in place by delicate chains of gold drawn about her hips.

"Are you deaf?" the newcomer demanded shortly. "Or don't you understand Greek?"

"You startled me," Leah said politely, finding her voice. "I am Leah of Petra."

"The girl who is to dance tonight? The nomenclator told me there was a peasant girl here, but you are hardly what I expected." She came closer and touched the palla. "Why haven't you undressed? They will be calling for you as soon as I finish." Without waiting for an answer, she sat down at the dressing table, elbowing Leah aside.

"I am dressed already," Leah protested as the newcomer began to paint her lips with carmine from one of the jars, laying on the scarlet dye with a brush.

"In that?" The other girl put down the brush. "They will laugh you out of the room. Or maybe not." She stood up and untied the ribbon about Leah's waist. Skillfully she adjusted the narrow bands beneath the younger girl's breasts and tied the ends again. When Leah looked into the mirror, she saw with startled eyes that the silken fabric now clung intimately to the upper half of her body, sharply accentuating the contrast between the slenderness of her waist and the budding fullness of her bosom. Stooping, the other girl also set the folds of the stola artfully, creasing the fabric so that it fell in many tiny pleats from the waist in front, but clung snugly to the curves of her hips. "That is much better."

"You must be a dancer too?" Leah stated.

"I am a slave," the girl flung over her shoulder. "They call me Thetis."

"Do you dance in—in that, Thetis?"

The slave girl stood up and smoothed the transparent fabric over her hips. "When the men are drunk enough, they like to snatch at your robe while you are dancing. Look here." She came closer so that Leah could see how the fabric was held at her shoulder and waist by tiny silver clips, fragile and easy to loosen.

"One good pull and the clips open," she explained. "The garment unwinds without tearing."

"And you dance naked? Before men?"

Thetis laughed. "Has no man seen you naked?"

"Never," Leah cried in horror. "Not even Demetrius, my foster father."

"Then you must be a virgin."

Rich color stained Leah's cheeks. "Of course! I am only eighteen."

Thetis laughed harshly. "I was sold as a slave at twelve, and I gave birth at fourteen. Listen, little one," she said earnestly. "This is an evil place. Go back home and marry some nice Jew and bear him children. Believe me, the Jews are the only decent people I ever met."

"But all Romans are not evil," Leah protested.

"All I ever knew," Thetis said matter of factly. "Wait until you know what it is to be pawed by a fat man stinking of wine. Like those who are here." She threw up her head and listened. "That's my music." And adjusting the golden chains about her hips, she opened the door to the triclinium and shot through it, her body already writhing in the sinuous movements of her dance. A sudden burst of sound greeted her, with shouts, the clash of an overturned goblet, then the door swung shut, leaving the small room unnaturally silent.

7

L eah felt a sudden, almost overpowering urge to take herself away from this palace as fast as she could go. Tales of Roman orgies, heard second or third hand, were only juicy bits of scandal. But now she was face to face with reality; in a few moments, she must go into the next room and dance before shouting, drunken men. Only the thought of the thousand sesterces that had practically been promised kept her from running away then. She could not deprive Demetrius, she reminded herself, of the things tonight's purse, and the others that would follow if she succeeded here would mean to him. But she could not and would not compete with naked slave girls in sensuality, she decided firmly. Her dance must stand or fall upon sheer beauty.

Leah went to the door leading to the triclinium and cracked it open cautiously until she could see the room. Its size startled her; she had never seen a room for dining so large. At one end were the couches upon which the banqueters reclined, arranged around a huge table like the spokes of half a wheel. The other end of the room was cleared for the entertainment, and here Thetis was dancing to music played by musicians hidden in an alcove.

The triclinium itself was beautiful, the ceiling inlaid with colored marble, the walls painted with lewd scenes at whose frankness Leah blushed and turned her eyes away. Five couches were arranged around the marble table, from which the food had been removed now, leaving only wine goblets. Two slender, feminine-looking boys moved about with wine jugs, filling goblets as soon as they were empty. They were fair-skinned with painted cheeks and mincing gaits.

Domitian lay on one of the couches. Beside him was a heavy man with a weak-sinuous face and little weak eyes whom she judged to be Nero. The three other guests were older, and all quite obviously drunker than the host. One, a large man with gray hair, Leah recognized as General Burrus.

Domitian, strangely enough, did not seem to be drunk as the others. He was watching the dancer with bored eyes, occasionally sipping from the goblet in his hand. Once more, Leah was struck by his beauty. Reclining there, he might have been Apollo descending from Mount Olympus to revel with the mortals. But there was something repulsive about him, too, she thought, or perhaps it was only a part of her natural revulsion of his companions, the scenes on the walls, and the painted Greek boys.

Thetis was dancing to the throbbing rhythm of the music, and as she spun on the marble floor, dipping and swaying in rhythm, she moved closer to the banqueters. She laughed and eagerly clutched her dress as she leaped gracefully away, teasing them deliberately again and again. Once she came close to Domitian, darting away as he reached negligently for the spinning hem of her costume, then moving in closer again with what was, Leah thought, deliberate intention, as if she were flirting with him, daring him to seize her garment. He grinned at her but waited until she was almost touching his hands. Then with a quick movement like the striking of an adder, he seized the flimsy cloth in his fist and jerked. As Thetis had explained to Leah, the clips came loose. When Thetis darted away in mock surprise, the bombyx unwound itself from her body. Halfway across the room, she paused, fingers over her eyes in pretended embarrassment, her body unclothed except for the girdle about her loins.

A roar of laughter rose from the reclining men and a spatter of applause. Then as the music changed to a slower measure, Thetis lowered her arms and began to dance once more. Now she scarcely moved her feet. The expressive movements of the dance were limited almost entirely to her torso and her arms and hands, both repulsive and yet fascinatingly beautiful in its picture of animal passion, the age-old story of courtship, conquest, and fertility. Such a dance the Queen of Sheba might have done before King Solomon. Watching it, Leah felt her own body begin to quiver, while her cheeks grew hot and her pulse throbbed to the rhythm of the music.

The drunken revelers were beating on the table as the dance rose to its inevitable climax. "The girdle! The girdle!" they shouted.

It was a hoarse roar of passion whose sheer provocativeness frightened Leah, tempting her to flee. Yet at the same time, she could not take her eyes from the scene. Her heart was throbbing like the drum head being beaten in the alcove, thrusting blood into her face until she felt as if her cheeks would take fire.

"The girdle! The girdle!" The shouts grew more insistent as the writhing of Thetis body progressed to its inevitable climax. Strings and pipes wailed a sensuous rhythm against the throbbing of the unseen drum. On a crash of sound, the dancer's hands flashed down across her hips and came away bearing the fragile girdle in her fingers. She poised for an instant, then tossed it directly at Domitian, who alone among the men seemed not to be sodden with wine.

The handsome tribune was forced to dodge lest the golden shell strike him in the face. But he made no attempt to catch it, and it was Nero who scrambled on the floor and came up holding it triumphantly. "I have the girdle," he bellowed happily. "The girl is mine for tonight." Then Thetis turned and ran from the room.

Leah jumped back from the door to escape being bowled over as the angry slave girl stormed in. "You were looking," she cried, panting with anger and the effort of dancing, her eyes darting fire. "Did Domitian try to catch the girdle?"

Leah shook her head. "It would have hit him if he had not moved."

"You!" The dancer turned suddenly to face Leah, feet apart and hands upon her full hips. "He refused me because of you." In her anger, Leah thought the slave girl would strike her. "You with your clinging robes and your talk of being a virgin."

"You are wrong!" Leah protested. "I came only to dance."

Before Thetis could continue her tirade, a crashing chord of music came from the triclinium. In it, Leah recognized the tones of the great cithara played by Hadja as the introduction to her own dance. Now that the reality of entering the banquet hall was upon her, she felt herself grow faint with fear and excitement and swayed momentarily, unable to force herself to enter the other room. Were it not for the wine of mandragora Luke had given her, she knew that one of the fainting spells would be upon her. And right now, she would have welcomed anything that freed her from the necessity of going on. Then with a strong effort of will, she forced herself to be calm and put her hand to the door.

"A thousand sesterces! A thousand sesterces!" These words with the rhythm of the great cithara, calmed her fears and gave her strength.

"I will do this for Demetrius," she told herself. And with confidence, she opened the door and stepped out on the marble floor of the banquet hall to face Domitian and his guests.

# 8

As Leah dropped the palla, one of the Romans laughed. Remembering what Thetis said, she stiffened and flushed with anger, but as the music took hold of her body, she tossed her head defiantly and launched herself into the dance.

Her body was a vibrant poem in praise of the beauty of nature. She was the wind storming through the mountains, the roll of summer thunder, and the majestic flash of lightening heralding the storm. Again, she was the rain swelling the taut skins of the grapes and wetting the freshly tilled soil in preparation for the falling seed from the hand of the sower.

Next the scene changed under the merry sound of the pipes, and the glad song of the strings. Her slender, fragile, and lovely body in its silken draperies now began to tell the happiness of children playing on the rain-wet grass, reveling in, the coolness after the shower. The listeners could both see and feel the things her body and the music were saying, and even in their drunkenness, they could not but share some of the emotion she was portraying.

Now, so softly that it could hardly be noticed, the mood of the dance changed again. The sun was setting, and in the protection of the shadows a boy and girl, lovers, were meeting. Shyly at first, then with increasing boldness as hand reached out to hand and heart to heart, they told each other the story of their love, portraying in beauty through the movements of the slender form upon the dance floor. The beat of their pulse rose with their newly awakened awareness of each other; the elation of their spirits was in every step, every breath-taking lovely posture. Leah's head was thrown back and her lips were parted, her mouth tender and soft as she portrayed without words the story of young love, its tenderness, and finally its gentle surrender as the boy drew the girl into his arms and found her eager lips waiting for his own. As softly as it had begun, the music ended on the first sweet kiss, and Leah stood, lost in the mood she had created, poised like a delicate flower nourished by love itself and newly burst into bloom.

A roar of applause broke spontaneously from the audience as she sank gracefully to the floor, bowing before the couch where Domitian lay. From the folds of his robe, Domitian drew a small pouch and tossed it to the floor beside her. From its metallic clink,

Leah was sure it was filled with coins, perhaps even more than the thousand sesterces for which she had dared to come and dance. With a swift, graceful movement, she picked up the purse and, running gracefully to the back of the room where she could see the musicians in the alcove, tossed it to Hadja, who caught it expertly.

Now the Nabateans lifted their instruments again and Hadja struck his great cithara with a sweeping stroke that set every string to vibrating. It filled the room with a throbbing burst of sound, reverberating from the walls, and setting the beat for the other instruments, as the cymbalist crashed his polished metal disks together and stamped the scabella upon the floor, adding their booming rhythm to the sudden rush of sound.

This was the music of the wild desert dance Leah had performed upon the street leading into Rome, and with a quick movement, she loosened the silken shawl that covered her hair. It poured down upon her shoulders in a cascade of molten beauty against the pallor of her skin and the pure white silk of her pleated stolla. Poised there, she was indeed, as Hadja had named her, the "Living Flame," a pillar of fire to set a man's heart burning.

Then, her body swept up by the throbbing beat of the music, Leah began the whirling, stamping dance of the desert people, the wild nomads who rode on the swift winds of the sandstorms and bedded themselves under the palms wherever a patch of green marked and oasis in the broiling wasteland. The dance itself was too strenuous to last long; soon her movements were so swift that the befuddled eyes of the Romans could distinguish them no longer. At its end, she poised for an instant to receive the plaudits of the diners, then disappeared through the door into the dressing room.

Panting, all aglow with the thrill of her triumph, Leah leaned against the door. Thetis had gone and the room was empty. Nor would she have had it otherwise, for this was a moment to be experienced alone, the heady thrill of triumph that comes to an actress after a superlative performance. Moving over to the tall mirror, she stood before it for a long moment, savoring again the beauty of her lithe body. Her hair was tossed every way from the strenuous movements of the dance, and seating herself at the dressing table, she began to comb it with a fine ivory comb she found there.

Intent upon what she was doing, Leah did not realize that the door into the hall had opened, until her startled eyes saw reflected in the mirror the handsome face and tall form of Domitian.

"Do not be afraid, little one." The tribune smiled reassuringly. "I only came to tell you how well you danced and to bring you this." He held out another purse, also swollen with coins. Without taking her eyes off him, Leah took the purse, thanked him, and thrust it into the pocket of her dress hanging over a chair.

Domitian pulled up a cushioned hassock and sat at her feet. "Your dancing was truly beautiful," he said.

"You are very kind." Her smile was wary.

"I mean it," he protested. "You made Thetis look like a cow."

"Thetis is very pretty." Leah's eyes twinkled. "She was angry when you did not catch her girdle."

Domitian shrugged. "Who would look at her when he could see real beauty? Thetis has a fine body, but no soul. You have both and therefore are perfection in itself." Then he smiled. "Enough of compliments. You must be hungry."

In the excitement of getting ready to come to the villa, Leah had forgotten all about eating. Now she realized that she was starving, but the thought of going into the room with the drunken Romans repelled her, and she drew back from the door.

Domitian saw the involuntary movement. "Not in there," he assured her. "I have ordered a table in a room close by."

"But my musicians. They will be ready to return home."

"They are eating now. I told them you would have supper here."

Leah hesitated, but there seemed to be no harm in staying for a few minutes. Besides, it would give time for his drunken guests to leave before they do.

"Are you still afraid of me?" Domitian asked with a smile. "I am not a monster who eats up little girls."

She could not help laughing.

"The two purses you have will allay your fears. Besides you have four body guards, and big ones, too. They grow strong men in the desert."

Her fears were silly, Leah told herself as Domitian guided her along the corridor. And it was thrilling to be waited upon by such a handsome man.

The room into which Domitian ushered her was not large, but it was luxuriously furnished. Heavy draperies hung at the windows and were pulled shut to keep out the night air. A broad soft-cushioned couch half filled the room, and through the open door of a large closet, Leah could see rows of the rich purple and white uniforms worn by the wealthy officers of the Roman Army.

"Is this your bedchamber?" she cried in sudden alarm.

"Yes, but you need not be afraid," he assured her. "See, your supper is already here." He took a burning taper from a bracket on the wall and set about the room lighting other candles, until the chamber was ablaze with light. "There," he said smiling. "That should assure you of my good intentions." Leah lifted the silver cover of one of the dishes arranged upon a low table and sniffed the delightful aroma. "It smells good," she added reluctantly.

"Go ahead and eat," Domitian urged. "If I had worked as hard as you did tonight, I would be starved."

Leah hesitated no longer. Everything was here for a young girl to like, including foods she had heard of but had never tasted before. On one plate was strips of salted and smoked fish, tender radishes on tiny center leaves of succulent lettuce, and other dainties to stir the appetite. While she ate, Domitian turned his back to her and poured into a slender goblet a mixture of wine and honey, and a powdered substance.

There was also a large plate containing cena, the main part of the meal. Tender slices of roasted and spiced beef were garnished with rich and savory vegetables. And then a pastry studded with nuts making up the last part of the meal, the mensa secunda, so the Romans called it.

While she ate, Domitian sat on a cushion at her feet, lifting the covers of dishes as she sampled them, and pushing them aside when she was finished. Finally, when she could eat no more, Leah wiped her mouth and fingers upon a napkin of linen finer than any she had ever seen before and took a deep breath of sheer content. Perhaps it was the wine, or the heady effect of his admiration that made her feel dizzy. It didn't occur to her then that there might be another, a more dangerous cause.

"Did you like your supper?" he asked.

"Oh, yes. It was wonderful."

"And have I offended you at all?"

She smiled. "Of course not, but I must go now. My musicians will be wondering where I am."

He took her hand and pulled her to her feet. She was quite close to him, closer, she knew, than she should be. As he smiled down at her, his broad chest touched her body and she felt the softness of her flesh give way against him. Her breath seemed to stop in her throat. "I—I must go," she stammered, but she could not draw away.

"Don't I deserve at least a kiss as a reward?" He held her hands still in his. "After all, I did help you get the dance before some very high officials and they were enchanted with you, and their favor can mean much."

It was part of the thrill of adventure, even of danger, that characterized the evening. Besides, the purse he brought, plus the one she had tossed to Hadja, comprised money that had not been in the house of Demetrius for many years. And being generous by nature, Leah could not very well help feeling a warm glow of appreciation toward the handsome tribune who had made these things possible. After all, she told herself to quiet her pounding heart, there could be no harm in giving him a little kiss.

Domitian saw that she was tempted to yield and drew her gently to him. But when she would have given him her soft cheek, he claimed her mouth roughly and his arms tightened about her. Leah had seen passion in the eyes of men when she danced, but she had never been so close to it as this. Startled by the shock of Domitian's mouth upon hers, his hands upon her body through the thin silk of her dress, she was paralyzed for a moment.

It was a strange new feeling, this pounding of blood in her temples and throat, this constriction in her chest, this sudden whirling of her senses that was more than the effect of wine. Leah did not know what was happening at first, then she had a surge of revulsion and fear. Forcibly she broke away from the demanding caress of his mouth and pushed herself clear momentarily of his embrace, but the man who held her now was not the same one who had waited upon her so gallantly while she ate. His face, so handsome a moment before, was swollen and distorted by lust, and his eyes were wild and bloodshot, like one suddenly demented.

While she struggled in a sudden rush of terror to break away from him, Leah screamed again and again, but the thick hangings of the room dulled the sound. Her strength was failing fast, and what she felt now was the aura preceding a fainting spell.

Leah could only resist feebly when she felt Domitian lift her in his arms, for a strange paralysis was already upon her. She could no longer move her limbs, and when she tried again to scream no sound came, for her senses had already begun to lose contact with reality. Mercifully Leah of Petra became unconscious.

# 9

Luke was away when the nomenclator of Domitian called to request that he visit Lady Alphina who was staying at her son's villa while her husband Vespasian was in Israel. It was just before dark when Luke and Onesimus returned home and received the message from Paul.

Darkness had fallen by the time Onesimus tied their mule to a tree outside the villa of Domitian. As Luke was removing the nartik containing his instruments, medicines, and leeches from the mule's back, he noticed another mule and cart tied nearby, but paid little attention, for he was concerned lest Lady Alphina be angered by the slowness of her favorite physician answering the summons.

The boudoir to which they were admitted was small but exquisite. It was removed from the banqueting hall by some distance where the reveling had ended earlier. Alphina was like one of the delicate figurines from the countries beyond the Eastern Sea. Every line of her lovely features showed breeding, for she carried the blood of the Julio-Claudian line of Roman emperors. But there was also a warmth and understanding in her eyes. When Luke saw that she was not angry, he drew a sigh of relief.

"I was treating the sick and did not get the message of your nomenclator until an hour ago," he explained.

Alphina smiled, "I should apologize for making you come all the way across the city after dark. And who is this handsome young man you have with you?" she asked admiringly.

"This is Onesimus, my assistant. He is a big help to me. Now, how can I be of service to you?"

"The problem is here, with my left arm." She lifted a flimsy sleeve and exposed an angry red swelling in the upper part of her arm. Luke recognized the nature of the problem at once, for such conditions were not at all uncommon in his experience. An insect bite, a small pimple, then in a few days a painful swelling and fever that lingered for days, unless it ended by rupture and expulsion of the poisons.

"Can you do anything to relieve the pain?" she asked hesitantly.

Luke ran his fingers gently over the swelling. As he suspected from looking at it, it needed to be opened. "Hippocrates once said, 'Those diseases which medicines do not cure, iron (the knife) cures,'" he told her.

"The knife!" she gasped. "But there will be a scar."

"Not as much as if it ruptures and drains by itself. And it will get well much more quickly if I incise it."

"Do it then," she urged. "And quickly. I have not slept for two nights."

"You will sleep tonight." Luke promised as he opened his instrument case.

Testing his scalpel with his thumb, Luke found it still razor-like sharpness for he honed it each morning before leaving his house. From the nartik, he also took a pad of washed wool and spread out a clean towel beneath the inflamed arm. Then he nodded to her that he was ready. She set her teeth firmly in a soft red lip, and he plunged the blade quickly through the thin red skin. Her gasp was more at the gush of bloodstained matter that burst from the abscess than from pain, for the thinned-out skin had little feeling in it. Luke slit the skin well across the top of the swelling, laying it wide open so that it would not be sealed off again before all the poisonous material could drain out.

"Was that so bad?" he asked as he bound a pad of washed wool expertly over the wound.

"Oh, no. I never thought anything could bring relief so quickly."

"If you will have your maid bring a little wine," he suggested, "I will mix you a sleeping draught. Then you can be sure of a good night's rest."

Alphina ordered the wine. "And bring a tray for the physician, and his assistant, too, Letha," she added. "I'll wager you two hurried here without eating."

Luke admitted that they had, and while he waited for the draught to take effect, he and Onesimus devoted themselves to the excellent food.

Luke's heart was light as Onesimus untied the mule in the grove outside the villa, for he had been well paid for the nights work.

Seeing the other mule and cart still tied to a tree as he led his animal from the grove, Onesimus wondered who might be visiting the villa at this late hour, but gave it little thought.

Then as he walked through the grove, a strange sound came to his ears. It was an odd noise, as if a man were groaning in pain. While he listened, it came again, apparently from the bushes near the river.

Leaving the mule with Luke, Onesimus searched until he found a branch and gripped it in both hands, approached the spot from which the groan had come.

Thieves often lay in wait for the late traveler along these roads, he knew, and a favorite stratagem was to pretend to be injured, luring the sympathetic wayfarer within reach of a long knife or a sword. It might be wiser not to stop at all, considering the value of the purse they were carrying.

Soon he made out a white form lying in the ditch. It stirred and a man's voice implored. "In the name of Ahura-Mazda, help me or I die."

The voice seemed familiar, and when he came closer, Onesimus recognized the swarthy face with its hawk-like profile and graying beard and the white robe stained now with mud. It was Hadja, leader of the musicians who played for Leah of Petra. The Nabatean appeared to be semiconscious.

Quickly Onesimus called to Luke. Luke knelt and ran his fingers over Hadja's skull, noting with relief that there was no depression of the bone. A cut over the injured man's temple showed that he had been bludgeoned, a serious injury if the bone were driven down upon the brain. The blood was sticky with some clotting, so it could not have been very long since he was wounded. The pulse Luke noted, was slow and strong, so he judged that no mortal wound was involved.

From his belt, Luke took a small flask of wine that he carried for emergencies such as this. The Nabatean swallowed automatically when the flask touched his lips, then gulped the wine when he realized what was being offered him.

"What happened to you, Hadja?" Onesimus asked.

"Is that you, Onesimus?"

"Yes."

"Praise be to Ahura-Mazda! She whom you love is prisoner in the villa."

"Leah?" Onesimus cried. "But how?"

Hadja told him then of the summons to the villa, of Leah's dancing before Domitian and his guests, and of her great success. "Afterward," he continued, "we were told by the tribune that the Living Flame was dining with him and we were to wait, but they served us food and led us from the palace under guard."

The stories he had heard about Domitian went racing through Onesimus's brain. "Why did you leave her?" he demanded angrily.

"Two soldiers with drawn swords walked beside each of us. I tried to break away, but one of them struck me down with the butt of his sword."

There was no point in blaming the Nabatean. Only by the rarest sort of luck had the soldier used the butt of his sword instead of the blade, leaving Hadja alive. Onesimus forced aside, too, the burning rage against Domitian that rose within him, for he must think clearly now. There might still be time to save Leah if he could somehow gain entrance to the palace again. Since the high walls precluded any entry by that route, there was only one way, the gate by which they had just emerged. The guard might remember that they had just left the villa and let him in.

"I'm going inside to get her," he told Luke.

"They will kill you." Luke warned.

"That is the chance I must take. Take your mule and go while you can." The musician stumbled to his feet, but swayed and was forced to catch hold of a sapling to keep from falling. "I am but a blind man who must be led," he mourned. "Take this knife, Onesimus. You may be able to slip it between the ribs of a Roman. I will wait for you here."

When he approached the gate, the guard stopped him with his sword. "What now leech?" he demanded. "Were you not well paid? I remember a purse hanging from your friend's belt."

"I left some of my medicines in the apartment of the Lady Alphina," Onesimus said, adding a silent prayer that the Most High would forgive him the lie. "Her maid knows me, so it will not be necessary to disturb anyone else."

The guard shrugged, and let him pass.

Two corridors opened from the atrium, which for the moment was empty. One, Onesimus knew, led to the apartment of Alphina, for he had just come that way, so he chose the other. Onesimus hurried along the corridor until he was stopped by a closed door, which he opened carefully. The room was empty, but a woman's dress that he recognized as Leah's was hanging over a chair.

Throwing the dress over his arm, he started out into the corridor but, hearing the creak of another door, drew back just in time.

While Onesimus watched, Domitian emerged from one of the rooms, staggered across the atrium and out of sight. Quickly now, Onesimus opened the door through which the tribune had emerged and stepped inside. A glance told him it was the Roman's bedchamber, for his sword and insignia lay in a chair. Then his eyes moved to the bed and he recoiled in horror, for a single glance revealed what had happened here. Leah was still unconscious, but her naked body, the pitiful tatters of her clothing in a pile on the floor where Domitian had dropped them could only mean that she had been ravished forcibly, in spite of her struggles to defend herself.

Onesimus knew that he must act rapidly, for the tribune might return at any moment. He quickly slipped on her the dress he carried over his arm. He then ripped a heavy drapery from one of the windows and wrapped it about her body to protect her against the chill of the night if they were lucky enough to escape the villa. All the while his thoughts were racing as he tried to decide what to do.

Going over the wall was out of the question. They were much too high nor could he leave the way he had come, carrying an unconscious woman in his arms. One avenue remained then, the river. He had no way of knowing how deep the water was at the end of the wall where it entered the river, but he must try to wade around the end of it. And if it was too deep he must swim, bearing the unconscious girl in his arms.

His decision made, Onesimus lifted Leah from the bed. Then carrying her in his arms, he stepped out upon the close-cropped green lawn outside. The way seemed to be clear now, and moving quickly, he darted across the open space to the protection of the ten-foot wall with steps leading down to the water. No outcry had risen yet to show that he had been discovered, so he crept beside the outer wall, steadying himself against it until his feet splashed in the water and a chill shot though his ankles. The chill of it threatened to paralyze him as he waded deeper, pressing his body against the wall in case he stepped off into a deeper spot and needed something to cling to.

Wading was difficult, for he had to hold Leah high enough so that she would not get soaked by the icy river water. The water reached his waist, then his armpits. A few more steps and he must swim. Then suddenly there was no more wall against his side, and with a thrill of exultation, he knew that he had reached the end. Turning sharply around the end of the wall, Onesimus felt the bottom begin to shelve up as he waded ashore on the outside. A few yards more and he was out of the water, staggering up the bank toward the path where he had left Hadja, with Leah's unconscious body in his arms.

The Nabatean had recovered enough to bring the mule and cart down the path to Onesimus. Leah still showed no sign of consciousness when he placed her on the rough floor boards of the cart, but although both were staggering from exhaustion, they wasted no time in leaving the villa, knowing the alarm might be given at any moment.

As they pushed along the road, Onesimus explained to Hadja only that Leah had suffered one of her fainting spells and that he had found her in a room in the palace. Hardly half a mile beyond the villa the road branched. The fork to the left ascended the hills past the great aqueduct bringing water to the city. The road to the right, however, went back into the city. They were turning to the left, thinking it might be a safer way back when Hadja said suddenly, "Wait, Onesimus! I hear something behind us."

Onesimus stopped at once. For a moment, he heard nothing. Then faintly, he detected the sound which had first reached the keen ears of the desert man, the sharp ring of metal on metal.

Such a sound could have many causes, but only one was likely tonight, the ring of a sword on a shield.

Hurriedly they worked the cart and animal off the road and out of sight among the trees. The terrain was rough, but a fringe of trees grew just beside the road. There they crouched, with a reassuring hand on the bridle of the mule, lest the animal stir and betray their presence. By the time they had hidden the mule and cart, the rattle of harness and the rhythmic tread of leather-shod feet were plainly audible. Shortly a party of soldiers with torches came into view, but without pausing at the fork, they wheeled to the right along the lower road leading into the central part of the city.

The two remained in the darkness beside the cart on which Leah's body lay, until the Romans were out of sight and earshot on the heights above, then worked the cart back to the road. Onesimus wiped his face and felt it damp with a cold sweat. Had not Hadja's sharp ears heard the soldiers in time, they would have taken the lower road. Nothing, then, could have saved them from capture, for the road below was narrow, with no way of getting the animal and cart into hiding.

"They must be going to the house of Demetrius," Onesimus stated. Then a thought struck him. "Do you know where Priscilla lives?"

"Yes, I have been there many times."

"Good, we will hide Leah there until it is safe for her to return to her place."

Hadja agreed. "Priscilla will be glad to give her shelter and take care of her."

With Hadja riding the mule and Onesimus walking beside the cart, they made their way to the house of Aquila and Priscilla.

# 10

Onesimus stirred and sat up, rubbing his eyes. The sun was already bright upon the floor of Priscilla's house, but Leah still lay on the couch where he had placed her when they arrived around midnight. He had spent the night stretched out on a quilt on the floor, where he could hear if she stirred from her stupor.

Aquila and his wife Priscilla had accepted without question Onesimus's story that Leah had been dancing for Domitian and had fallen in one of her fainting attacks. Hadja's wound proved superficial, and after Onesimus dressed it, he had been dispatched with the mule and cart to reassure Demetrius of Leah.

The sun was shining brightly, and the myriad of small, intimate sounds that went with an awakening household made last night seem only a nightmare. But when Onesimus looked down at the girl sleeping on the couch and saw the dark angry bruises upon her neck and arms when she had fought against Domitian, he knew in a sudden rush of concern that her own tragedy was very real indeed. Leah's hair was tumbled about her face and shoulders, and some color had come back into her cheeks, but her very helplessness as she lay there set a flood of tender concern rising within him. He wanted to take her in his arms and comfort her, letting her awaken in a safe haven that could always be hers if she wanted it. But she could not have heard these things had he been able to say them, and so he contented himself only with bending down and kissing her upon the forehead.

When he raised his head, he saw that her eyes were open, staring at him with a puzzled expression. "This is Priscilla's house," she whispered. "How did I get here?"

Onesimus gave her a quick account of his finding Hadja outside the villa and how he had taken her from Domitian's bedchamber.

"You know what happened then?" It was barely a whisper.

"Yes, but no one else does."

"Why didn't you leave me there to die?" she said piteously. Suddenly she began to weep. Great tears spilled from her eyes and ran down over her cheeks, but her face remained a frozen mask of suffering and shame.

Onesimus looked away. He sensed that nothing he could say would diminish her agony now. It would do no good to tell her that others had survived an equal desecration and had gone on living. He could not possibly know, as kind and understanding as he was, what the terrible experience meant. Only a woman who had been through it all could know that. But he could see how, overnight, the gay and carefree girl who had danced and sung for the sheer joy of it would never be the same.

The change was not only physical; it went deeper than mere flesh, into her very soul, a wound that would never completely heal. Not that she was outwardly changed, except for the bruises upon her body and the lines of suffering in her face. There was the same pale beauty, the same rich sheen in her hair, the same lovely body outwardly unchanged by the desecration it had survived. And yet the girl weeping there was an entirely different person from the gay and joyful Leah of Petra.

Finally the tears ceased to flow. "No one knows what happened last night except us, Leah," Onesimus said, trying to comfort her.

"I did not tell Hadja, or Priscilla. You must try to forget it: the memory can only bring you pain."

"Then let it," she said with sudden anger. "Where was God when I cried out to Him to save me? Why did He not answer me then?"

Onesimus was silent. Most of the devout Jews would have said God had deserted her as a punishment for her sins. But what was sinful about the desire to be happy and share one's happiness with others?

"You think I deserve it, too, because you told me not to go to the villa," Leah accused, lashing out like a child in her pain, instinctively trying to ally the hurt and guilt she felt through hurting another.

"None of those who love you could ever think or say such a thing, Leah," he told her gently.

"Why don't you go away and leave me alone?"

"Do you want to tell Demetrius anything?"

"Tell him I want to die." Her voice broke then the tears began to roll once more. "Tell him to forget he ever had a daughter," she whispered, and turning over suddenly, buried her face in the pillow.

Onesimus found Priscilla and warned her to watch Leah closely. Then, his heart heavy with concern for the girl he loved went to the house of Demetrius. There he learned that the soldiers had visited Demetrius during the night, seeking Leah, but had departed without troubling him when satisfied that she had not come there. The rest of the musicians had drifted in during the early hours of the morning, but the pudgy lyre maker had been worried until Hadja arrived with the news that Leah was safe.

"What really happened at Domitian's villa, Onesimus?" Demetrius asked soberly. "I am sure Hadja didn't know the whole story."

Onesimus had no alternative except to tell the truth. When he finished, Demetrius's face was set with grief and self-accusation.

"It is my fault," he said miserably. "I should have forbidden her to go."

"You were sick in bed," Onesimus reminded him. "And you know her spirit; she would have gone anyway."

"How is she now, Onesimus?"

"Like another person, cold and hard. I think the only thing that will carry her through all this is her determination to be revenged."

"What a terrible experience that must have been to a sensitive girl like Leah. Bring her back to me as soon as you can, Onesimus. Perhaps I can help her through this ordeal."

Onesimus shook his head, "I don't think any of us can really help her, Demetrius, as much as we love her. She must stay with Priscilla until we know whether or not Domitian will try to find her. When Luke goes back to dress Lady Alphina's arm, perhaps he can learn something of Domitian's plans."

Luke approached the villa of Domitian with some trepidation, for he could not be sure how much was known of his part in last nights happenings.

The nomenclator showed him to the apartment of Alphina. She was in very high spirits, for the pain had vanished almost magically. "Tell me the news of Christians, Luke," she begged. "I have been inside so long because of this arm that I have lost all touch with your people."

"There is talk of a dancer who was cruelly treated in this very house last night," Luke said as he applied the bandage.

"What do you mean?"

"She was invited to dance before the guests of your son Domitian. Afterward the musicians were removed from the palace by soldiers while the girl was held against her will."

"Was she harmed?" It was almost a whisper, and the color had drained from her face.

"The girl came here a virgin. But she is no longer."

"Not Domitian...?" she gasped. "He promised us this would never happen again." Then she composed herself. "My son is a fine soldier and a favorite of the emperor. But when he takes too much wine, he sometimes becomes like an—an animal, at least where young girls are concerned. My husband Vespasian will want to pay the girl and her family well, Luke. Do you know her?"

"My assistant Onesimus that you met yesterday had asked her to become his wife," he said simply.

Alphina gasped. "Luke, how terrible!" She put her hand gently upon his arm. "Is there anything I can do?"

"Domitian sent soldiers to pursue her when she escaped last night," Luke explained, "but she is in a safe place. Naturally she is devastated and hates all Romans."

Alphina nodded, "I can understand her hating us. What has all this done to Onesimus?"

"It is hard for him not to desire revenge."

"I cannot blame him for that," she agreed. "But he would only lose his own life. Rome does not always send its best representatives abroad, Luke, and things like this only makes us hated even more. But Vespasian would never have condoned this. I can assure you on one thing," she continued. "Domitian will not harm the girl again. He sails in a few days for Alexandria. He is to train Roman troops and will be gone for several months."

This was good news indeed, for then Leah could go back to her home and no longer hide from her betrayer. Luke hurried out of the villa to carry the news back to Onesimus and Leah.

# 11

Leah came home to the house of Demetrius a few days after it was learned that Domitian had departed Rome, but there was little improvement in her spirits. She remained in her room most of the day, or sat in the garden holding her beloved lyre, yet never touched the strings. Nothing Demetrius or Onesimus could do seemed to lift her spirits. She said nothing to show her feelings, speaking only when spoken to.

And so the weeks past. Then one day, Leah appeared at Paul's house early one morning. Paul and his guard had gone to market, and Luke and Onesimus were about to leave to visit patients. Leah's eyes had a strange glow, and she seemed excited about something. Luke's immediate reaction was that she might have a fever, but when he questioned her, she denied feeling badly at all. "I came to get more of the wine of mandragora," she explained. "My bottle is empty."

Onesimus noticed that Leah was looking at a large jar at the end of the shelf. "My fortune," he explained with a smile and lifted it down. "See, the coins fill it almost halfway now. I have been saving practically all my salary."

Leah lifted a handful of gold and let it trickle through her fingers. "You already have enough to take you anywhere you want to go," she stated.

While Luke filled her bottle carefully from a large jug in which he kept his supply of this powerful and useful extract, Onesimus sat down beside Leah and spoke to her. "Is it news to you, Leah," he said gently, "that I love you and want to marry you?"

"Don't, Onesimus," she whispered. "Please don't." She sank down on a bench and put her face in her hands. Yet when he would have comforted her, she only pushed him away. "Go on to your patients," she whispered finally without looking up. "I will wait here and talk to Paul when he returns."

Reluctantly, he took up the nartik containing Luke's instruments and medicines and left the house. Their first visit took almost an hour, while Luke applied leeches to the swollen eye of a wool dyer. When it was finished, they hurried back to their house, for they did not like the idea of Leah's being there alone when she was so much disturbed.

The house seemed empty until they went into the surgery room to drop the leeches that were fat with the dyer's blood into the tank and get fresh ones before leaving for their other calls. And there they found Leah, lying unconscious on the floor, with the empty bottle that had contained the wine of mandragora beside her.

For a moment, Onesimus could not believe what he saw. It seemed incredible that Leah would have tried to take her own life when that very morning, she had shown more animation than she had for a long time. But then he remembered their conversation several weeks before, when Luke had told her of the power of the mandragora root to produce sleep and death.

Why had she done it? Onesimus asked himself as he picked up her limp body and carried her to the couch in his own room. She was still alive, but from the limpness of her muscles and the slow, shallow breathing, he was sure that a large amount of the drug must already have entered her body. He could have understood her trying to kill herself in the agony of shame following her experience at the hands of Domitian. But almost two months had passed now, time for the shock to wear off and let her become somewhat adjusted.

Luke wasted no time. Only a little more than an hour had elapsed since they had left her, he calculated, so even if she had taken all of the drug at once, there was an excellent chance that some remained in her stomach. If he could remove that, it would at least have no further power to harm her.

Fortunately he carried in his bag a kulcha, or stomach tube. What followed was not pleasant, but when he finished he had the satisfaction of knowing that at least a part of the drug she had swallowed was removed. Next he used the tube to put into Leah's stomach a liberal dose of an antidote. He then wrapped Leah in a blanket while Onesimus heated rocks on the cooking hearth to add more warmth. Everything possible had been done to remove the poison.

Through the day and into the evening, Onesimus remained beside the couch where Leah lay. The harsh cast of suffering in which her features had been set for the past weeks was relaxed now as she lay unconscious, and she looked once more like the happy girl he had first loved when he saw her dancing in the street. Seeing her lying there sleeping peacefully, he found it even harder to understand what had made life suddenly so unbearable for her that she had tried to kill herself.

For a while, as the day receded into the shadows of the night, it seemed that Leah's spirit would leave her body. Desperately Luke fought to save her, expending all the resources of his skill and his stock of stimulant drugs. Finally, he and Onesimus fell on their knees beside the couch and prayed that God would let her live, and as night settled over the city, Luke felt the pulse under his fingers grow stronger. With a rising sense of exultation, then he knew that he had won his battle with death.

It was after midnight when Leah showed signs of returning consciousness. Suddenly she started writhing, seemingly in pain, drawing up her knees as if trying to find a comfortable position. And when Luke put his hand on her body through the covers where the pain seemed to be centered, he could feel a tension in her abdominal muscles. Seconds later they relaxed and she stretched out her limbs, but almost immediately the spasm came again. This time, she moaned and he thought for a moment that she was regaining consciousness, but the spasm ended and the lines of pain in her face were erased for a short time, until another bout began. Now, however, Luke was able to make the diagnosis, and at last he understood why Leah had tried to kill herself. When he told Onesimus, he was shocked.

How long since she first realized that she carried the child of Domitian within her body, he could not know. But it must not have been more than a few days, he judged, for she had conceived less than two months before. Now he understood how knowledge of her pregnancy the past few days had been more than she could bear.

The forces of nature worked rapidly once they had begun, but fortunately Leah herself was still too deeply under the effects of the drug to be conscious of the pain or even of what was happening. When it was all over, Luke removed all traces of the formless incubus and Onesimus buried it in the garden.

It was morning before Leah awakened. She was pale, and great dark shadows showed beneath her eyes, but Luke could see no other effects of the ordeal through which her body had passed. Onesimus had remained beside the couch all night and he was there when she awakened. "Everything is all right, dear," he reassured her. "I found you in time."

Slowly her face assumed its former harsh cast. "I wanted to die," she said bitterly. "Why did you stop me?"

"No one has the right to take his own life, Leah. You must live for those who love you."

"And be labeled a harlot when I bear the child of Domitian?"

"That is what I am trying to tell you," he said gently. "The conception has been expelled; your nightmare is over and no one knows of it except Luke and me."

For a long time she did not speak. Leah turned her face to the wall then and Onesimus did not try to say anything more to her. Finally she turned back to him and her eyes met his, and the look of determination in them startled him.

"I will not try to kill myself again," she said slowly and distinctly. "Now I have something to live for."

For a moment Onesimus dared to let himself hope she could mean what he wanted so much to hear her say. But her next words dashed his hopes.

"Today I swore to the Most High a solemn oath," she told him. "An oath that I will not stop until I have killed Domitian and am revenged."

Nothing Onesimus could say had any effect upon her decision. In vain, he pointed out that her resolve could only end in unhappiness, perhaps in death. But Leah's fiery Jewish blood had triumphed over the more logical Greek in her heritage, harking back to the implacable laws of Moses, when God had said, "Thou shall give life for life, eye for eye, tooth for tooth, hand for hand, foot for foot, burning for burning, wound for wound, stripe for stripe."

Leah improved rapidly over the next several days. She had sent to Demetrius for her lyre and strummed it off and on during the day, sometimes singing songs Onesimus had never heard before. But he did not delude himself into believing this was the same Leah of Petra he had first come to love. A demon of hate that would not let her rest until she had accomplished her purpose through the death of the man who had defiled her body.

# 12

The rise of Poppaea Sabina's position as mistress and virtual ruler of Emperor Nero's emotions had been accompanied by the development of an entirely new structure of political power within the imperial household. General Alfranius Burrus, the most admired and loyal military figure in the empire, had consistently opposed Nero's plan to divorce his wife Octavia, and marry Poppaea. But with Poppaea pregnant and demanding that her child have the legal status of succession in the empire, Nero finally dared to defy Burrus.

Certain now that she had the upper hand over her imperial lover, Poppaea first arranged with her conspirators for Burrus to be poisoned. Next, Octavia was banished to the island of Pandatiri on a trumped-up charge of adultery and shortly killed—rumor even saying that her head was cut off and deposited in bloody cloth at the feet of Poppaea.

Knowing that the new empress was in league with many influential Jews in Rome and that, through her, their opposition to him might lead to his own assassination, upon some trumped-up evidence, Paul decided to take a step he had so far avoided and appeal to the one man who still seemed to have some influence over the emperor, the philosopher Seneca. To this end, he sent a letter to Seneca asking for an appointment, citing as a reason for the request, the fact that the philosopher's younger brother, Gallio, had once judged him innocent of any crime in Corinth. Not long after the letter was sent, Paul received a courteous invitation from Seneca, asking him to come to his home.

Though Seneca had been a tutor of Nero and, with Burrus, one of the most powerful men in the empire through his influence over the young emperor, he still lived in the same rambling structure he had inhabited before his rise to power. It was a typical Roman house, with an open court, or atrium, in the center of which water from a pipe poured into a shallow pool. Paul and his guard, with Onesimus, were ushered into the atrium and directed to seats upon a bench beside the pool by a slave in charge of announcing guests of his master. Through the open door of another room, the apostle could see racks of scrolls and judged that it must be the philosopher's library.

While they were waiting, a door opened on the other side of the atrium and a young woman entered. Her hair was dark and she wore a simple white robe, with strands of pearls about her neck. Against the background of the shrubbery planted around the pool, she made a picture of quiet beauty that was refreshing, after the overdressed and over painted women who thronged the streets of Rome.

Paul and Onesimus got to their feet and the rattle of chains attached to Paul's wrist warned the young woman that she was not alone. Startled by the presence of intruders, she first turned to the door from which she came but, seeing Onesimus and Paul with his guard were there, came around the pool toward them. "Forgive my rudeness, please." Her voice completed the picture of quiet loveliness. "I didn't know anyone was here."

"The nomenclator told us to wait," said Paul.

"Then Seneca knows you are here?"

"Yes." Seeing her eyes go to the chain bonding him to the guard, the apostle said, "My name is Paul of Tarsus. I am awaiting trial before the emperor."

"Are you the Paul who preached in Asia?" The young woman's eyes brightened with interest when he spoke his name.

"Yes."

"I have relatives there; they mentioned you in letters. I am Claudia Acte."

"The emperor's mis—Forgive me. I have no right to judge."

"I was honored to be Caesar's concubina. He gave me my freedom."

The story of how Seneca and Burrus had deliberately stirred Nero's interest in the lovely young slave woman, hoping her quiet goodness and devotion would have a controlling effect upon his often tumultuous passions, was well known throughout the empire. But Acte had been put aside when she was unable to compete for Nero's rather fickle attention with the wanton charms of Poppaea Sabina. And though she had not been destroyed like Octavia or General Burrus, she had been banished to a villa at Velitrae, where she lived in quiet seclusion. Knowing all this, Paul was surprised that she had risked invoking the wrath of the Empress Poppaea by returning to Rome.

"A freedom you will not enjoy much longer, if you are foolish enough to come to Rome again." The speaker, a gray-haired man with the lined face and deep-set eyes of a scholar, stood in the door to the library. Acte ran to kiss the old man on the cheek and his face softened as he put an arm about her waist and moved across the atrium toward where the men were standing.

"Forgive me for keeping you waiting," he said to Paul. "In your letter, you mentioned that you were a native of Tarsus. Gallinus tells me you are a Jew remanded for trial from Caesarea by Procurator Porcius Festus because of offenses committed in Jerusalem."

"Yes, I was born in Tarsus," Paul explained. "A large Jewish colony has been there for many years."

"Since the time of Antiochus Epiphanes, I believe," said Seneca. "That would account for your being a Roman citizen. In what way can I help you?" The old philosopher took a seat upon a bench and Claudia Acte sat beside him. Paul and his guard, with Onesimus, resumed their seats upon a bench near the pool.

"I have been in Rome for almost two years awaiting trial before Caesar," Paul explained. "My accusers have not yet come forward—"

"A common trick where the case is weak. An unscrupulous man can bury another in prison merely by not making charges against him."

"I was hoping you might use your influence with the emperor to have my case brought up for trial, so I may be free to go on with my work," said Paul.

"You have chosen a frail reed to lean on, my friend," said Seneca. "The same evil companions who turned the favor of Nero away from this lovely child are slowly weakening any influence I ever had over him. One day I shall be found dead in my bed—of poison, as was my friend Burrus, or with my veins open."

"They wouldn't dare harm the greatest mind in Rome!" Acte cried indignantly. "Caesar would have their heads."

"Not if it is by his order," Seneca said briskly. "I only hope that when the time comes, you will not share my fate—as you certainly shall if you come here again. Your place is at Velitrae."

"My place is with Nero—if he needs me," Acte said quietly. "I can't believe he ordered General Burrus poisoned."

"You and I have lost, my dear. We cannot help Nero—even though we love him for what he could have been. Our task now is to save ourselves—if we can."

During the exchange, Seneca and the girl seemed to have forgotten the presence of their guests. Unwilling to add to his troubles and theirs, which were certainly large enough, Paul got to his feet.

"I hope you will forgive me for coming here, noble sir," he said. "It was an impertinence."

"Nothing is an impertinence—if it gives one man the chance to save his soul by helping another," said Seneca. "Please sit down and tell me why you were accused by the Sanhedrin?"

"Actually, my case was never heard before them. The chief captain of the garrison at Jerusalem sent me to Caesarea because of a plot to assassinate me."

"By whom?"

"The chief priests—and others."

"Why would they want to kill you?"

"Because I preach a doctrine they will not accept. And because the death of the man I serve is upon their conscious."

"The man you serve?"

"Jesus of Nazareth, the Messiah promised to the Jews."

"You are a follower of Chrestus?"

"A Christian, yes." Paul was familiar with the Roman version of the word Christ. "But I have broken no law of Rome."

"Can you prove your innocence?"

"I proved it long ago—before your brother in Corinth."

"Tell me more about that," said Seneca. And Paul described briefly his appearance before Gallio and the Proconsul's refusal to listen to the charges against him.

"If what you say is true, the Christians are only a sect within the Jewish faith, as my brother ruled, and the Imperial Court will no doubt set you free."

"I'm sure my accusers know that," Paul agreed. "Which is probably why they haven't come forward to present their case."

"Tell me more about the worship of Chrestus," said Seneca. "I have never had the opportunity to study it."

Seneca and Acte had listened closely through the long story of Jesus's ministry, his crucifixion and his resurrection, the calling of Paul himself on the road to Damascus, and his subsequent ministry until the time of his arrest.

"Where have you found the greatest response to your preaching?" he asked. "Among your own people or those you Jews call Gentiles?"

"Gentiles. Almost everywhere I have gone, I have been turned away from the regular Jewish synagogues."

"And in Rome?"

"I have failed here too." A spasm of pain crossed Paul's face. "Not only do the Jews refuse to listen to me, but I have made few converts among the Gentiles."

Onesimus listened intently. Hearing the disappointment in his voice, he could not help feeling empathy for the old man. There was also a sense of guilt and conviction on his part, for he had not yet made a decision to embrace the Christian faith.

"I would have told you all this would happen—if you had come to me with your story when you first reached Rome," stated Seneca.

"But why?"

Acte responded. "I came from Asia and my family is part Greek," she continued. "Your faith has a great appeal to me, especially now that I have so little to cling to. But to a Roman, it's too mysterious and set upon to high a plane. That's why you succeeded so well in the East but found so little response elsewhere."

"Exactly what doctrine were you preaching in Galatia and in the Greek provinces?" Seneca asked.

"I preach Jesus as the Messiah promised by the scriptures and sent to bring salvation—"

"To Jews only?"

"To all who will believe and accept him."

"A Greek or Roman with no previous knowledge of a Messiah— or what the word means—would have trouble understanding at the very beginning," Seneca objected.

"Many have failed to understand," Paul admitted.

"Things of the spirit are always hard for most people to understand," Seneca agreed. "If that weren't true, there would be no need of philosophers."

"I spent some time once in a Christian family before I entered the emperor's household," said Acte. "They were Jews, who had left Jerusalem because of persecution—"

"Probably one I carried out myself, before the Lord called me," Paul admitted.

"They believed Jesus of Nazareth was the Messiah sent to the Jews, but I heard nothing about this doctrine you preach of Justification through faith in him."

"I was about to ask you that," Seneca said. "Don't you preach a different doctrine from what was taught by disciples of the Nazarene after he was crucified—and by Chrestus himself?"

"I preach only what has been revealed to me," Paul insisted'

"That may be," Seneca agreed. "After all, who knows by what path a man reaches a final conviction. In any event, I think I see now why you have been able to appeal so strongly to those whose background is Greek. And why you have failed so utterly with those who are Jews—or Romans."

"Tell me the answer if you have it," Paul begged.

"We Romans are a practical people. After all, we still worship Apollo and Zeus—yes even emperors—although intelligent Greeks long ago either gave up religion altogether or began searching for the sort of fulfillment through spiritual effort you seem to have gained through serving your Christ."

"You aren't like that," Paul protested. "Yet you are a Roman."

"A Roman, yes—I've devoted my life to a purely Greek form of philosophy, that of the Stoics. We Romans control most of the world, but we still haven't forced Roman ideas and cultures—if we have any on those we conquer. I strongly suspect that if the Romans are to be known for anything important in the history of the world, it will be for helping spread Greek thought, knowledge, and culture to the farthest ends of the earth. This has been a most interesting discussion, Paul of Tarsus. I hope you will come back to see me again, so we can talk further about it."

"And my trial?"

"I don't know what I shall be able to do about that. After all, I'm almost completely out of favor in the emperor's household. But I still have friends who are indebted to me in other areas of the government. Perhaps they can see that the imperial courts decide to hear your case soon."

Paul had to be content with that. As he was leaving, Claudia Acte walked them to the door leading to the street. "I cannot help you, but I think you can help me," she said to Paul. "Could you possibly come to Velitrae and talk to me more about this faith of yours? It isn't safe for me to come here often."

"I cannot leave Rome, but I have an associate who would be glad to come. I shall send Timothy to see you," Paul promised. "And I hope you will become one of us."

"What I have been in the past would hardly earn me the favor of your God of old," she said. "But your Christ is forgiving and I need a faith now to sustain me in what lies ahead. I think I found that today."

# 13

Since their arrival in Rome, Mark and Timothy had been teaching Christians in the catacombs, but mostly in individual homes. Because Paul had earned the trust of his guards, one by day and one by night, he was allowed to go to the catacombs and teach with the guard remaining outside the entrance. Although Onesimus had known of this place where Christians buried their dead and of Paul teaching there on occasion, he had never been to it.

Late one afternoon, Timothy insisted that Onesimus go with him to the catacombs to hear Paul teach. It lay across the river from the imperial palace. And since this area was easily reached by way of bridges crossing the river from the central part of the city, Christians spent considerable time there.

As they approached the entrance to the catacombs, several people were making their way carefully toward the entrance. Some carried lanterns. The Roman police could not enter the underground graveyard because of Roman law, so Christians were safe here.

As they entered the opening, more and more torches gleamed. The number of people grew greater. Some of them sang in low voices, which seemed to Onesimus filled with sadness. At moments, a separate word or phrase of a song struck his ear. At times the name of Christ was repeated by men and women. Some, passing near, said, "Peace be with you!" or "Glory be to Christ!"

Walking slowly with others, they finally came into a huge circular room filled with a great throng of people. Near the crept, ignited torches had been pitched into a pile and made a glowing orange light. After awhile, the crowd began to sing a certain familiar hymn, at first in a low voice, and then, louder. Onesimus recognized it to be a hymn he had once heard in the home of Philemon of Colosse. A strange yearning struck his heart, a kind he had never known before. At Timothy's suggestion, they sat down beside one of the pillars used to support the ceiling.

Eyes turned upward, the people seemed to see some one far above, and with outstretched hands seemed to implore him to descend. When the hymn ceased, there followed a moment as it were of suspense—so impressive that Onesimus looked up at the high ceiling, as if in dread that something uncommon would happen and that someone would really descend to them.

Onesimus had seen a multitude of temples of various structures in Asia. He had read about many religions, most varied in character but, here for the first time, he saw people calling on a divinity with hymns—calling with a genuine yearning which children might feel for a father or a mother. One had to be blind not to see that his companion Timothy and the others honored and loved their God.

Meanwhile a few more torches were thrown into the fire, which filled the huge room with ruddy light. At that moment, an elderly bald-headed man entered the room. This slight man mounted a stone which lay near the fire. It was the Apostle Paul.

The crowd swayed before him. Some knelt, others extended their hands toward him. There followed a silence so deep that one heard every charred particle that dropped from the torches. It seemed to Onesimus that the form which he saw before him was both simple and uncommon. The old man had no crown on his head, no garland of oak leaves on his temples, he wore no white robe; in a word, he bore no insignia of the kind worn by priests—oriental, Egyptian, or Greek. And Onesimus was struck by that same difference again which he felt when listening to the Christian hymns.

Paul seemed to him, not like some high priest skilled in ceremonial, but as it were a witness, simple, aged, and immensely worthy of respect, who had journeyed from afar to relate a truth which he believed. There was in his face, therefore, such a power of convincing as truth itself has. And Onesimus, although he had prior conversations with Paul about the Christian faith, he remained a skeptic and did not wish to yield to the charm of the old man, yielded, however, to a certain curiosity to know more about Jesus.

Meanwhile Paul began to speak, and he spoke from the beginning like a father instructing his children and teaching them how to live. He enjoined them to endure persecution patiently. He said they are to love one another and bear each others burdens, to be just, pure, and peaceful, that they might live eternally with Christ after death, in such joy and such glory, in such health and delight, as no one on earth had attained at any time.

And here Onesimus could not help but notice that there was a difference between the teaching of the old man and that of Cynics, Stoics, Agnostics, and other philosophers; for he taught a magnificent glorious life. He spoke of it as certain.

Onesimus wondered about all this. What he had just heard was difficult for him to understand. At the same time, he had a feeling that there was something mightier than all other philosophy's. He thought it was impracticable, but because of its impracticability, it was divine.

Onesimus thought of all this through the medium of his love for Leah. Yes, he loved her. He had never felt this way about any other girl. Then he thought of Domitian. Would she really try to kill him? He would be in Alexandria for several more months. Would she go there or wait upon his return to Rome? He felt a sudden compulsion to leave. He wanted to see Leah.

Timothy glanced over at him and smiled. The quarry man added more torches to the fire. Paul continued to talk about Christ, his death, burial, resurrection, his ascension, and his coming to earth again. A silence set in which was deeper than the preceding one, so that it was possible, almost, to hear the beating of hearts. He talked about having seen Christ and being changed by the power of God. The remembrance of his encounter with Christ brought tears to his eyes, which were clearly visible by the flickering light of the fire. His glistening hairless and aging head was shaking, and his voice died in his breast. Paul closed his eyes, as if to see distant things more distinctly in his soul, and continued.

Onesimus listened, and something wonderful took place inside him. He forgot for a moment where he was; he stood in the presence of two impossibilities. He felt that it would be necessary either to be blind or renounce one's own reason, to admit that Paul who said "I saw" was lying. There was something in his movements, in his tears, in his whole personality, and in the details of the events that he related which made every suspicion impossible.

To Onesimus, it seemed at moments that he was dreaming. But round about, he saw the silent throng. The odor of smoke came to his nostrils. At a distance, the torches were blazing. And before him on the stone stood an aged man near the grave tunnels, with his head trembling somewhat, who, while bearing witness, repeated, "I saw! I saw!"

Paul began to invite people who would place their faith and trust in Christ to step forward and make that decision. Several stood up and began walking toward Paul. In the faces of those present were evident happiness, joy, and expectancy. Many went forward kneeling before Paul praying.

Rome did not exist for those people, nor did the Emperor
Nero or his persecution; there were no temples of pagan gods;
there was only Christ, who filled the land, the sea, the heavens, the
world, and the hearts of those who invited Him into there lives.

Onesimus felt Timothy's hand upon his arm and found
himself walking toward Paul. Convicted and broken, he received
Christ into his heart, and Onesimus became a Christian.

After leaving the catacombs, Paul persuaded his guard to
stop at the river where he baptized Onesimus and the other
converts. With the conversion of Onesimus, there was great joy
and celebration in the Christian community. But happiest of all
was Leah, who embraced him when he told her of his conversion.

The next morning at breakfast, Onesimus told Paul of his
secret. "I have been wanting to tell you something for some time,
especially now that I am a Christian." He paused and then said:
"I am a runaway slave from Colosse."

Paul put down a piece of fruit that he was eating and looked
at Onesimus. "But you have no holes in the lobe of your ears that
mark slaves," he stated.

"I was a teenage boy when my parents were sold to the owner
of a silver mine in Perga. Some slave owners only mark their
slaves when they become adults. I was fortunate in that regard,"
Onesimus explained.

"I ministered in Colosse some time ago. What was your
master's name?"

"Philemon."

"Philemon?" Paul repeated excitedly. "I know the family. In
fact, he and his family are converts of mine. I baptized the entire
family. What do you think you should do?"

"I have learned much from you over the last several months,
and my heart tells me I need to go back to Colosse and ask
Philemon's forgiveness," Onesimus admitted.

"It is the right thing to do," Paul stated. "Philemon is indebted to me. When you decide to go back, I will write a letter for you to take and present to Philemon. You are a brother in Christ and should be treated as such. I'm sure he will be forgiving. Let me know when you plan to leave."

"Thank you, Paul," he said gratefully. "I will let you know soon."

# 14

Paul was bitterly disappointed that the passage of time seemed to bring him no nearer an opportunity to plead his cause before the Imperial Court and gain his freedom. Eager to leave Rome and plow what he believed would be fertile fields in Spain, he fretted continually at the delay, until Luke was afraid he might endanger his health.

One thing did bring Paul a great deal of satisfaction—the conversion of Claudia Acte to the Christian faith. She required little persuasion, after the morning spent in talk with Paul and Seneca. Timothy visited her several times at Velitrae, and one day, she came to the outskirts of Rome so Paul himself could baptize her as a Christian.

Though Paul often felt a sense of irritation at Seneca for what appeared to be inaction, as far as speeding up his trial was concerned, he could not know that the old philosopher was actually working slowly to accomplish just that. By speaking a word here and talking with an old acquaintance there, Seneca managed finally to bring the case to the attention of the Imperial Court.

The trial itself was something of an anticlimax. Held before one of two praetorian prefects—Nero was much too occupied with the new forms of debauchery to which Empress Poppaea and her cronies had introduced him, plus his singing and flute playing, to be troubled by such unimportant legal chores. The hearing proceeded rapidly to its inevitable conclusion.

The charges forwarded by Festus were in three categories, each was heard separately. First, Paul was accused of disturbing the ritual of the temple at Jerusalem, a charge he easily refuted by the testimony of Luke who, being a Greek and a respected physician in the praetorian camp, was well known to the judge. Second, he was accused of desecrating the temple, but since no representative of the priestly hierarchy appeared to condemn him, that charge, too, was summarily dismissed. The third accusation, that of being the leader of a sect that conducted treasonous activities against the empire, was potentially a capital offense and therefore far more serious than the others. To it, Paul devoted the major part of his defense.

He cited first the decision of the magistrates of Philippi not to persecute him on a somewhat similar charge brought by the owners of a slave girl. Then he went on to the account of his hearing before Gallio who, as a proconsul and the brother of Seneca, was well known and respected in Rome. Finally, he cited a statement made by Herod Agrippa II and Festus just before his departure from Caesarea that, had he not appealed to Caesar in order to save himself from the danger of assassination, he might have been set free.

All of this, plus the failure of the Jerusalem authorities to produce any tangible evidence against him, weighed heavily in the final decision. Paul was declared innocent of all charges that very day. The chains he had worn for almost four years, beginning at Caesarea, were struck off, and free at last, he could turn his face to the west. Before leaving, however, there was still much to be done in Rome. Needless to say, the Christian community in Rome celebrated Paul's freedom.

The disturbing news came from Jerusalem that James, the kinsman of the Lord, had been arrested and brought before the Sanhedrin. After only the briefest of hearings, he had been seized by the temple rabble and cast down the outer steps of the sanctuary. There, his body already broken, he had been stoned by the mob until he was dead.

Simon Peter was not in Jerusalem any more, so the Christians there had chosen as the new leader of the Church—Simeon, the son of Cleophas, and like James, a kinsman of Jesus's family. Paul was tempted to go there and strengthen the small community, but Silas and Luke persuaded him against such a course, since it might appear to the Roman authorities that he had gone back to cause trouble in an area that was now in a state bordering upon open rebellion.

Peter had been traveling among the cities and churches in Pontus, Galatia, Bithynia, and Capadocia and had recently arrived in Rome. For months, Mark had been writing all that he could remember of Peter's teachings. Luke had also been recording the Acts of the Apostles from Paul's teachings. Both were in hopes that sometime in the future, their words might be read in the churches throughout the Roman Empire.

The sales of the Cithara that Leah's workman were producing under the supervision of Demetrius had slowed considerably. And so it was decided that they would once again return to the streets of Rome to provide income for food and rent of their house.

Leah had selected a street near the market place for their first performance. A large crowd gathered as she began singing and dancing. There were shouts of approval and applause as she finished, and the sound of coins clinking at her feet as Hadja picked them up.

Mark and a large man who looked familiar to Leah approached her, and seeing that it was Peter, she ran to him and embraced him. "Before Demetrius, Simon was the first person who had ever been kind to me in my whole life," she told Mark.

Peter looked at the great crowd and recognized an opportunity to preach. As he was speaking, some Greeks interrupted and began to argue with him, and a scuffle broke out.

Sometime later, Leah rushed into her house plucking the shawl from her head so that her hair tumbled in a glorious torrent of living copper about her shoulders. In her excitement, she did not see Onesimus and Luke. "Demetrius! Demetrius!" she cried. "I brought Simon; he has been hurt."

Several people followed Leah into the garden. The tall musician, Hadja, was supporting a veritable giant of a man in the garb of a fisherman.

When Onesimus ran to help Hadja ease the fisherman down on a bench, Leah saw him for the first time. "I just came from your house, Onesimus," she cried in astonishment. "Paul said that you and Luke would not be back until evening."

"I sent for them," Demetrius explained. "I could hardly breathe and feared for my life."

"I'm glad that you and Luke are here," she said to Onesimus thankfully.

"It's good to see you, Simon," Demetrius said as he struggled to breath. "What was the disturbance this time. As I remember, you Galileans are always first in the fighting."

"Some Greeks were arguing that the Jews will not rule the world when the Messiah comes," Simon explained. "We broke a few heads, but one of them had a club. You are the only sensible Greek I ever saw, Demetrius."

"Because I know better than to argue with you, my friend," the lyre maker said. "Now sit still and let Luke examine that gash above your eye."

Luke knelt beside the injured man and cleaned his wound. From his pouch, Luke measured out a dose of dried poppy leaves and mixed them in wine. Simon drank the mixture with a grimace. While he waited for the drug to take effect, Luke began to prepare his needle and horse hair to close the wound. In a matter of minutes, the wound was closed and bandaged.

"Is he going to be all right?" Leah inquired.

"Yes," replied Luke. "I have done what I could, but healing comes from the Most High."

"What about Demetrius?" Leah asked.

"I examined him before you arrived. Liquid keeps building up in his body putting pressure on his lungs and heart. I can drain it off, but it will come back. I'm afraid there is little more that can be done."

"No!" Leah exclaimed. "I cannot lose Demetrius."

"Now Leah, dear," Demetrius assured her. "I'm not dead yet. We've been through some hard times together, and we will get through this one."

Leah walked Luke and Onesimus to the door, and when it was opened for them to leave, Onesimus saw an orange glow over the city. Rome was on fire.

# 15

Word spread quickly throughout the Christian community. There was excitement everywhere. To Onesimus, it seemed at first glance that not only was the city burning but the whole world, and that no living thing could save itself from the ocean of flame and smoke.

"If the fire reaches here," Onesimus said to Hadja, "take Leah and everyone to the catacombs where they will be safe. Luke and I must hurry to our house and see about Paul. I will come back after we get Paul to a safe place."

As Onesimus and Luke made their way across the north side of the city, light from the fire filled the sky as far as human eyes could see. The moon rose large and full from behind the mountains and took on the color of heated brass. In the heavens, rose-colored stars were glittering, but the earth was brighter than the heavens.

They met increasing numbers of people fleeing from the central part of the city. People with bundles on their backs, mules and carts laden with personal effects, liters in which slaves were bearing wealthier citizens. And as they neared the praetorium, the streets became so thronged with people that it was difficult to push through the crowd.

In the general uproar, it was difficult to inquire about anything. People to whom Luke asked either did not answer, or with eyes full of terror answered that the city and the world were perishing.

As they continued, more and more men, women, and children flooded the streets from the direction of the fire, increasing the disorder and outcry. Some sought desperately those whom they had lost. Smoke now filled the streets, making it hard to breath.

Onesimus learned from one man that the fire had started at the Circus Maximus, but extended with incomprehensible rapidity and seized the entire central part of the city. The entire circus was burnt, as well as the shops and houses surrounding it.

"This is no common fire," the man said. "I saw men hurling burning torches into buildings. People are crying that the city is being burned on command of Nero. Many are perishing in the flames. This is the end of Rome!"

From the sea of fire and smoke came a terrible heat, and the uproar of people could not drown the roar of flames. In the midst of this surging throng of humanity, wild and unrestrained, Asiatics, Africans, Greeks, Thracians, Germans, howling in every language on earth, came the praetorian guard, under whose protection the more affluent population had taken refuge.

Onesimus had seen captured cities but never had his eyes beheld a spectacle in which despair, tears, pain, groans, rage, and license were mingled together in such chaos. Above this heaving mad human multitude roared the fire sweeping through the city and up the hill tops of the greatest city on earth.

Finally, making their way through the throng of people and smoke, they arrived at their house to find Paul standing looking toward the flames and the screaming people running away from it.

"Paul!" Luke shouted, "we must hurry and take from our house clothes, food, your scrolls, things we might need in case the fire reaches here." Loading the cart and mule, they headed for the catacombs.

The concern for Onesimus was not for himself, but for Leah. But with Hadja, Peter, and the others, she would be protected, and this gave him some comfort.

Families lost one another in the uproar; mothers called on their children despairingly. At times, new columns of smoke from beyond the river rolled toward them, smoke black and so heavy that it moved near the ground, hiding houses and people as they pushed toward the bridge leading to the catacombs. Smoke pained the eyes and breathing was difficult. Even the inhabitants who, hoping the fire would not cross the river, had remained in their houses so far, began to leave them; and the throng increased. Onesimus remembered that the house of Demetrius was surrounded by a garden and beyond the garden, an unoccupied space. This thought consoled him. The fire might stop at the vacant space.

Finally, toward morning, they reached the catacombs. It was already filled with people. When Paul was settled safely, Onesimus told Luke he must go back for Leah.

"It would be impossible for you to make your way back across the city," Luke stated. "They may have fled their house already. My advice is to get some rest and wait for them here."

"I suppose you are right," agreed Onesimus, "but I worry about her safety."

The next day, there was no sign of Leah and her group. Meanwhile the dreaded element was embracing new divisions of the city. It was impossible to doubt that criminal hands were spreading the fire, since new conflagrations were breaking out all the time in places remote from the principal fire. From the heights which Rome was founded the flames flowed like waves of the sea into the valleys densely occupied by houses; houses of four and five stories, full of shops on the bottom floor. In those places, the fire, finding an abundance of inflammable materials, took possession of whole streets with unheard-of rapidity.

People camped outside the city, or standing on aqueducts, knew from the color of the flame what was burning. The furious power of the wind carried forth from the fiery gulf millions of burning shells of walnuts and almonds, which, shooting suddenly into the sky, like countless flocks of bright butterflies, burst with a crackling, fell on other parts of the city.

All thoughts of rescue seemed out of place; confusion increased every moment. The population of the city was fleeing through every gate to places outside. The shout "Rome is burning!" did not leave the lips of the crowd. It was repeated most generally, however, that Caesar had given the command to burn Rome, so as to free himself from odors which rose from the city, and build a new one under the name of Neronia. Rage ceased the populace at thought of this.

It was said also that Nero had gone mad and that he would command the praetorian guard to fall upon the people and make a general slaughter. Others swore that wild beasts had been let out by Nero's command. Men had seen on the streets lions with burning manes and mad elephants trampling down people in crowds. There was some truth in this, for in certain places elephants, at site of the approaching fire, had burst out of their containment and gained their freedom, rushing away in wild flight, destroying everything before them like a tempest.

Public report estimated at tens of thousands the number of persons who had perished in the conflagration. In truth, a great number had perished. The fire began in so many places at once that whole crowds of people, while fleeing in one direction, struck unexpectedly a new wall of fire in front of them and died a dreadful death in a deluge of flame.

Hardly a family inhabiting the central part of the city survived; hence along the walls, at the gates, and on all roads were heard howls of despairing women, calling out names of loved ones who had perished in the fire. From the sea of fire shot up to the heated sky gigantic fountains, and pillars of flame spreading at their summits into fiery branches, and swept them toward the Alban Hills.

The hapless city was turned into one pandemonium. The conflagration seized more and more space, took hills by storm, flooded level places, drowned valleys, raged, roared, and thundered.

Knowing that Leah might be in danger, it was not easy for Onesimus to stay in the catacomb, especially since Leah's group had not arrived. He remembered the difficulty he and Luke had in getting Paul here. Leah, he thought, must be in trouble.

"I must try and find Leah," Onesimus declared. "If I die, I die, but I must try."

Luke did not protest.

Onesimus knew he could not go back the way he had come. He resolved, therefore, to go around the city and cross the river beyond the fire. He had no idea how long it would take him to arrive at the house of Demetrius. Taking a sack of food and water, he mounted Luke's mule and headed south. At some point, he knew he would have to cross the river and make his way around the city itself. After two days, exhausted from the journey and lack of sleep, he finally reached the house of Demetrius. It stood untouched by the fire. As he rode up to the house, he glanced heavenward with thankfulness though the very air full of smoke burned his lungs. He pushed the door open and rushed in. The house seemed quite empty. "Perhaps they were overcome by smoke," thought Onesimus. He began to call—

"Leah! Leah!"

Silence answered him. Nothing could be heard in the stillness save the roar of the distant fire.

"Leah!"

Leah did not answer his calls, but she might be in a faint. Onesimus sprang to the interior. The atrium was empty and dark with smoke. Feeling for the door which led to the sleeping rooms, he found no one. He quickly went through the house, and even the cellar. It was evident that Leah and the others had sought safety elsewhere.

And then a thought came to him. Many Christians under persecution would secretly go north of the city to the sand pits for prayer and worship. The hour had come now in which he must think of his own safety, for the river of fire seemed to pursue him, as he made his way east before heading north to the sand pits. Exhausted, he failed to recognize the street along which the mule stumbled. He had not slept for two days, and it seemed that consciousness was leaving him gradually. He remembered only that he must find Leah. And all at once, he was seized by a wonderful certain conviction, like a vision before death, that he must see her, marry her, then die.

The exhausted mule staggered from one side of the street to the other. Finally coming to the path that led beyond the gardens of Agrippina, he made his way toward the hill. For a while, the slope of the hill concealed the conflagration. He turned still to the left and saw swarms of gleaming lanterns.

"She has to be here," he thought. Then he heard singing, and the lanterns were vanishing inside a dark opening. Suddenly Onesimus found himself amid a whole assemblage of people. He dismounted, tying his mule to a bush, and entered the excavation. Lanterns and torches were burning. By the light, Onesimus saw a whole throng of kneeling people with raised hands. He could not see Leah, the Apostle Peter or Hadja, but he was surrounded by faces solemn and full of emotion. Light was reflected in the whites of their upraised eyes. Some were singing hymns, and others were feverishly repeating the name of Jesus.

Meanwhile the hymn ceased. Then it was silent. From a distance was heard the crash of a house falling from being consumed by fire. But most Christians took those sounds as a visible sign that the dreadful hour was approaching; belief in the early second coming of Christ and in the end of the world was universal among them. Terror seized the assembly. Many voices repeated, "The day of judgment! Behold, it is coming." Some covered their faces with their hands. Others cried, "Christ, have mercy on us!"

But there were faces that showed no fear. At moments, however, silence came, as if all were holding their breath, and waiting for what would come. And then was heard the distant thunder of parts of the city falling in ruins.

Suddenly a roar louder than any had preceded shook the quarry. All fell to the earth. Silence followed, and in places weeping of children. At that moment, a certain calm voice spoke above the prostrate multitude—

"Peace be unto you!"

That was the voice of Peter the Apostle, who had entered the cave a moment earlier. At the sound of his voice, terror passed at once, as it passes from a flock in which the shepherd has appeared. People rose from the earth; those who were nearer gathered at his knees, as if seeking protection under his wings. He stretched his hands over them and said—

"Why are you troubled in heart? Who of you can tell what will happen before the hour comes? The Lord has punished this Babylon with fire, but his mercy will be on those who believe, and you whose sins are redeemed by the blood of the Lamb will die with His name on your lips, but you will rise again to eternal life. Peace be unto you"

Peter's words fell like a balm on all present. Instead of fear of God, the love of God took possession of their spirits. A feeling of solace possessed the whole assembly, and comfort, with thankfulness to the Apostle, filled their hearts and they knelt at his knees.

# 16

Onesimus approached Peter and, kneeling before him, said, "Lord, I have sought her in the smoke of the burning and in the throng of people; nowhere could I find her, but I believe that you can restore her."

Peter placed his hands on the head of Onesimus. "Have faith, my son," he said, "and come with me."

They left the crowd and turned into another ravine, at the end of which a faint light was visible. Peter pointed to it and said—

"There is the hut of the quarry man who gave us refuge."

The hut was rather a cave rounded out in an indention of the hill and was faced outside with a wall of reeds. The interior was lighted by a fire. Some dark giant figure rose up to meet them, and inquired—

"Who are you?"

"Servants of Christ," answered Peter. "Peace be with you, Hadja."

Hadja bent to the apostle's feet; then recognizing Onesimus, embraced him. "Blessed be the name of the Lamb, and for the joy of seeing you again."

As they entered, Onesimus saw Demetrius sleeping on a bed of straw. Near the fire sat Leah with a string of fish, intended evidently for supper. Occupied in removing the fish from the string and thinking that is was Hadja who had entered, she did not raise her eyes. But Onesimus approached, spoke her name, and stretched his hand to her. She sprang up quickly then; a flash of astonishment and delight shot across her face. Without a word she threw herself into his open arms.

He embraced her, pressing her to his bosom for sometime. Then, withdrawing his arms, took her temples between his hands, kissed her forehead, her eyes, and her lips. He repeated her name and embraced her again. His delight had no bounds as she clung to him.

At last, he told her how he had searched for her at the walls, in the smoke at her house, and how terrified he was of not finding her.

"But now that I have found you, I am overjoyed." He then turned to Peter. "Rome is burning at command of Caesar. And if he has not hesitated at such a crime, think what may happen yet. Who knows that he may not bring in troops and command a slaughter of Christians. He may even accuse them of setting fire to Rome."

Outside, from the direction of the city, as if to confirm his fears, distant cries were heard full of rage and terror.

"I want you to stay here for a couple of days until the storm passes. I can see you need rest. Stay until you get your strength back." Pointing to Leah, Peter said, "Then you can take the maiden, whom God has predestined to you, and save her. Let Demetrius and Hadja go with you."

After they had eaten, Onesimus thanked Leah for the meal. He then stretched out on Leah's pallet and instantly fell asleep. Having been deprived of sleep for two days, he slept well into the next day.

On the sixth day, when the fire had reached empty spaces, it weakened. Burned houses, however, fell here and there, and threw up pillars of sparks. But the glowing ruins began to grow black on the surface. After sunset, the heavens ceased to gleam with bloody light, and after dark, blue flames quivered above the black ash.

The banks of the Tiber were covered with drowned bodies, which no one collected; these decayed quickly because of heat heightened by fire and filled the air with foul odors.

"Did you say our house was spared?" Leah asked Onesimus.

"Yes, the fire died out in the open space before your house."

"Then we must go there before vandals invade the place. We cannot stay up here forever. We can put Demetrius on the mule and the rest of us can walk," she pleaded.

"Where is Peter?" asked Onesimus.

"He took Mark and left to see about Aquila and Priscilla. Their house, as well as many Christians, is on the outskirts of the city. Perhaps their house was also spared."

The next morning, they made their way to the house of Demetrius. To their surprise, Leah's musicians were there, having lost their home in the fire. There was a joyous reunion, and seeing that Leah was protected and safe, at her insistence, he left to see if Luke and Paul were back home.

To his amazement, their house near the praetorium was still standing. Upon entering the house, he found Paul and Luke who had come from the catacombs the day before. After a joyful embrace, Onesimus told them of Leah and the others.

"I have just come from the praetorian guard quarters," Luke stated. "I was summoned there to care for some who had burns." Then the look on Luke's face told Paul and Onesimus that he had brought grave tidings indeed.

"Do you know how many of our people were hurt during the fire?" asked Paul.

"Not many, but those who burned to death were fortunate. The persecution that is to come will be far worse than the flames.

"Why would Christians be persecuted because fire happened to break out in Rome? The whole central part of the city has been a fire trap."

"I learned that the people are crying for vengeance. The enemies of Nero first sought to put the blame on him, but Nero saw a way to escape his own guilt by shifting the blame to Christians. I have been told by a very reliable source that Nero has ordered the arrest of all Christians and to be put in underground prisons to await the games and gifts he has promised to the angry populace. Nero has also ordered the praetorian guard to round up slaves to clear all debris from the central part of the city and to construct an arena in which to slaughter Christians. All Christians need to be warned of this. They must be extremely careful and stay in their homes until the storm passes."

"It has ever been the way of the tyrant," Paul agreed.

"Onesimus and I need not be as concerned about our safety as others. As a physician and Onesimus as my assistant, we will be protected by praetorian guards as we seek to minister to the physical needs of so many victims of the fire. In fact, the government has set up several clinics around the city to meet the needs of the populace. I have been assigned such a medical clinic in the southern part of the city."

"When will we be leaving?" asked Onesimus.

"As soon as we can pack our supplies and pick up two praetorian guards to go with us," stated Luke.

"But I must warn Leah and others about the danger of this new persecution of Christians," demanded Onesimus.

"I understand, you can leave at once, but take the mule and hurry. We will leave as soon as you come back," Luke said sympathetically. "The first wave of persecution has already begun. My friend at the praetorium said that Christians will be hunted down and seized everywhere. He told me that they will be thrown to wild beasts. Others will be nailed to posts along the streets, their bodies doused with oil, and set afire as human torches."

"Onesimus, try to find Peter. He needs to know about this," informed Paul.

"He and Mark were going to the house of Aquila and Priscilla when I last saw them a few days ago."

"I need to tell you one more thing before you go," Luke said reluctantly. "When our enemies heard Peter was in Rome, they arrested him yesterday and accused him before the emperor of being a leader of the Christians. Thank God Mark is safe."

"Is he still in prison? Perhaps I can go and plead—"

"Peter is dead, crucified by Nero with his head down at his own request—lest he seem to emulate Jesus," Luke said sadly.

Sized by a sudden vertigo at the shock of what Luke had told him, Paul swayed and might have fallen had not Onesimus taken him by the arm and guided him to a couch. Pouring a cup of wine from a flask on a table nearby, Luke held it to the apostle's lips while he drank.

"I was afraid something like this would happen when you heard the news," he said.

After a few minutes, Paul's color returned, and when Luke felt for the pulse at his wrist, it was regular and strong.

"Doesn't Seneca have any influence on Nero?" Paul asked.

"Seneca retired to his home to think and write. But Poppaea and Tigellinus accused him of being a part of a plot to dethrone Nero in favor of Vespasian and the emperor ordered Seneca to kill himself by opening his veins."

"I shall pray for his soul. He never became a Christian, but he was very close to believing. And he was a good man."

"Many good men have perished on Nero's orders."

"What about Claudia Acte?"

"As far as I know, she is still in Velitrae—and safe. There was talk in the praetorium that the emperor wanted Claudia Acte as his mistress once again, but she refused."

"Then she held fast to her faith?"

"I'm sure she did, but it still may cause her death. Everyone agrees, Nero is like a mad dog turned loose upon all who dare oppose him—particularly Christians.

# PART III

# ALEXANDRIA

# 17

There was a great need for physicians in Rome, especially after the great fire that destroyed the old central part of the city. The government had set up clinics for those who had need of a physician. Luke was asked to go to the extreme southern part of Rome. It would be too far for him to come back to his house each evening, so arrangements were made for him to stay at the clinic. He was to be there for one week and then be relieved by another physician. Luke had asked Onesimus to go with him as his assistant.

"Luke and I will be leaving for a clinic that has been set up in the extreme southern part of the city. He says we will be gone for about a week. He is packing the cart and will be ready to leave as soon as I return. I just wanted to tell you good-bye, and be sure you tell others about the persecution. Will you be all right?" Onesimus asked Leah.

"I will be fine," she said. "There is no reason you should worry about me. Didn't Luke say that Domitian is still in Alexandria?"

"Yes," nodding his head. "I understand he is to be there for several more months. But I am concerned about you because I love you."

"I love you, too, and I will miss you," she replied sadly, and kissed him.

Luke was ready and anxious to get started on their journey. He had packed everything that they needed for their trip. Soon they were off with Luke riding the mule and Onesimus walking.

A week elapsed before Luke and Onesimus returned home. While he was away, Onesimus thoughts were constantly of Leah. Now that he had embraced the Christian faith, he hoped Leah might look with more favor on his suit for her hand in marriage.

Upon returning home, he hurried to the house of the lyre maker. Onesimus reviewed in his mind the arguments with which he would bowl Leah over and convince her to marry him. He would even take care of Demetrius.

At first, he could not understand what was changed about the lyre maker's house when he approached it from across the street of the Greeks. Then he realized that he had heard none of the usual sounds with which the building ordinarily rang, the tapping of hammers on resonant woods, the sound of strings, and above all, a girlish voice of incomparable beauty lifted on the mountain air. His spirits suddenly doused by a sense of foreboding, Onesimus crossed the street and came up to the house. It was then that he saw the bars nailed across the doors and windows.

An old man passing in the street stopped. "If you are looking for the maker of lyres," he asked, "he has gone. He and all his household."

"When did they leave?" Onesimus cried. "Where did they go?"

The man shrugged. "A few days ago. I only know they traveled southward toward Puteoli."

"Was the girl with them? The girl called Leah of Petra?"

"The one with the red hair? Yes. She walked beside the mule that carried Demetrius." And then he cracked. "Or was it two mules? The lyre maker is too big for one."

Onesimus could learn no more, either from the old man or from the neighbors, but all agreed that Demetrius's party had gone southward, so he could be sure their destination must be Alexandria.

From Puteoli, a traveler could take ship almost daily for Alexandria, reaching it in a few days. Undoubtedly Leah had somehow persuaded Demetrius to go to Alexandria at once, and Onesimus was sure the decision was tied up with her oath of revenge for Domitian.

But why had she gone without telling him? And where had come the money for the trip? Even with the purses she had received for her dancing, she would not have had enough to take her, Demetrius, and the musicians, as well as the two skilled artisans of the lyre makers household, to Egypt.

Onesimus's every impulse urged him to follow Leah. By renting a fast horse or camel, he knew he could pursue them along the Appian Way and probably reach Puteoli before they took ship. Not that he could hope to persuade her to return; he knew Leah too well for that. But she might at least promise to wait for him in Alexandria. And after living in Egypt for awhile, she might be more willing to return to Rome as his bride.

Onesimus decided he would follow them and hurried back across the city to his home. It would take money to hire a camel or horse—they were much more expensive than the slower mules—but the jar in which he kept his coins held more than would be needed. He went to the shelf where he kept the jar that contained his savings. As he lifted it down, the jar seemed lighter than he remembered. But only when he turned it upside down and saw that no coins fell from it did the truth burst upon him.

Onesimus knew now where Leah had found the money to take her and the others to Alexandria.

Paul and Luke discouraged Onesimus from following after Leah. "Perhaps in a few months, she will tire of Alexandria and come back to Rome," Luke suggested. "My advice to you is to wait it out."

Reluctantly Onesimus agreed. After all, he had no money for the trip to Alexandria. He would save his salary for the next three month, he thought, and if Leah did not come back to Rome, he would go to Alexandria.

# 18

It had been a long lonely three months for Onesimus, but he was determined to find Leah. Mark had volunteered to accompany him to Alexandria, for his desire was to organize a church in that great city.

The long oars groaned constantly now in their leather collars, driving the vessel onward. And when he came on deck, Onesimus found the sea illuminated brightly although dawn had not yet broken. Captain Quintas told him they were ten miles from Alexandria.

The coast line of Egypt was so low in the region that the great city itself was not yet visible, but the lighthouse of Pharos was in full view, rising abruptly from the sea. From the low island on which it stood to the top of the giant mirror before which great fires were kept burning from the setting to the rising of the sun, the tower was nearly six hundred feet in height, a pillar of alabaster-white stone directed all mariners to Alexandria. And although the fires were dying down, the rays from the great polished mirror still blinded one momentarily if he looked directly at them.

Patterned after the Babylonian style of architecture, this tallest of the wonders of the world consisted of four stories, one atop the other, the lower ones square and the topmost circular. The blocks of stone were said to be welded together with molten lead, since nothing else would have been impervious to the salt spray that dashed high against its sides during the winter storms.

"I envy you the site of Pharos for the first time from the sea," Mark said. "It is not nearly as impressive from the Nile and Lake Mareotis when approached from that direction, as I did some time ago." They were standing on the bow of the ship while it breasted the surging breakers beating endlessly upon the shore, as if anxious to rush upon and engulf this city that was in Egypt. Behind them, the overseers strode up and down the catwalks between the benches where the galley slaves sat, each chained to the great oar that he pulled. If one oar failed to move exactly in cadence with the others, the whip cracked and there was the scream of pain. This seeming cruelty was not without reason, however, for a false move here could set the oars crashing into each other and send the ship, swinging suddenly under the unimpeded force of the long sweeps upon the other side, plunging to its death upon the rocks at the base of the great tower.

Then when it seemed that another sweep of the great oars would set them upon rocks, Captain Quintus shouted an order. The slaves on the eastward side banked their oars, and the great vessel swung sharply, thrusting its prow into a narrow passage between perilously craggy rocks jutting from the sea and the end of the great stone breakwater on the left. Like an arrow directed at a target, the great ship shot through the opening into the wide expanse of the harbor itself.

The transition from wave-tossed sea to the glassy calm of the great harbor was astonishing. In the protected quiet of the breakwaters, the water was as smooth as a pond. Onesimus could see white sand on the bottom and rocks here and there garnished with seaweed of various hues, swaying as gracefully as the slick dolphins cavorting in schools on the surface. Brilliant-colored fish, their hues rivaling the rainbow, moved about the depths, ignoring the great ship floating above them.

From the prow of the ship the whole waterfront of Alexandria was spread out before their eyes. Not even in Puteoli, for all its glory, had Onesimus seen anything approaching this sight in magnificence and sheer man-made grandeur. To the left, eastward as he faced across the harbor, lay the curving breakwater called the Diabathra, forming one boundary of the harbor. There the royal palace stood and close beside it, shining in the morning sunlight, was the temple of Isis. In the smaller and protected harbor, great barges lay at anchor, their gilded railings and colorful canopies gleamed in the morning sunlight.

The sails were lowered, and now the ship moved slowly across the broad expanse called the Great Harbor. The shore of the Great Harbor was lined with great stone quays to which were tied ships from all parts of the world. They were a district unto themselves, into which merchandise could be brought free of duty for transshipment to other lands. Thus Alexandria formed a most important focus in the distribution of goods and materials throughout the Roman Empire.

Onesimus had never seen so many ships. Merchant ships, coastal galleys, lighters, barges, rowboats, from which men seemed to be hawking everything under the sun—the masts were a forest, the bright-colored sails and pennants a riot of color.

Nowhere else in the world was there anything quite like this most colorful and interesting city, and Onesimus's pulse quickened just at the thought that at last he was here. The quays were thronged with people from every nationality, priests with long robes with strange hieroglyphs on their foreheads, Roman soldiers, faces, voices, and garments from every country in the world-all crowded the docks, milling about, it seemed, without purpose.

Most startling to Onesimus, however, were the women. They were everywhere here, darting between groups of men or hanging onto them in frank invitation, wearing flimsy dresses and faces shamelessly painted.

"We are docking in the Regia," Mark explained. "It is sometimes called the Royal Area and is one of the busiest parts of the city."

"I never saw such warehouses," Onesimus admitted. "Or so many people."

"They are even larger on the other side, on the shore of Lake Mareotis. Shipping from the Nile and from Persia and the coast of Malabar is handled over there. Wait until you see the grain barges," he continued. "The life line of Rome runs across this narrow tongue of land between Lake Mareotis and the sea upon which Alexandria lies."

Docking a vessel the size of the great round merchant ships from Rome was a tedious process, and the morning was half gone before Onesimus and Mark came down the gangplank. Their baggage was already piled upon the quay and a host of porters surrounded them, all jabbering at once. But Mark quickly selected two and gave them instructions where to take the baggage. A dozen sedan chairs waited to carry travelers into the city, but at Mark's suggestion they chose to walk the short distance to the Greek Quarter where they would stay for the time being.

Leaving the waterfront, they traversed the cool arcades of the Forum and found themselves upon the great central thoroughfare called the Street of Canopus. Flanked by rows of colonnades, this main east-to-west artery of Alexandria cut through the city in a straight line for over three miles and was more than thirty paces in width. The stone-paved ribbon led to the Gate of Canopus on the eastern side, where a canal led to the city of that name on still another of the many mouths of the Nile delta. Adjoining the Gate of Canopus, the Jewish Quarter occupied almost a third of the city, constituting the largest population group of this great metropolis.

The Greek Quarter was not simply for Greeks, but actually housed people from every nationality. Egyptians, Italians, Cretans, Phoenicians, Cypriots, Persians, Syrians, Arabs, Jews, Indians, and occasionally a slant-eyed citizen of the empire of yellow men far to the east walked the stone-paved streets and added to the babble of voices. However, only one language was common, the everyday Greek of the common people that nearly everyone spoke with one accent or another.

Finding Leah in this great metropolis was going to be far from easy, Onesimus realized as they traversed the teeming streets of Alexandria, for nearly half a million people lived within its boundaries. His first disappointment came the next day after his arrival, when he went to the famous theater, just off the waterfront, and sought word of her. He was refused admission to the director's presence, and his inquiries brought only the information that no such person as Leah of Petra was or ever had been employed in the Alexandrian theater. Huge posters displayed everywhere about the city announced that the darling of the Alexandrians, a dancer called Flamen, would perform in the theater every afternoon, with a group of dances never seen on any stage.

Hoping to learn something of Leah in the Jewish Quarter, Onesimus and Mark presented their letter of introduction that Paul had written for them to Philo Judaeus, the famed lawyer and leader of the Alexandrian Jews. They were received courteously and treated to spiced cakes and wine by the white-bearded patriarch who was counted the most influential Jew outside of Jerusalem. But even Philo could tell them nothing except that no one named Leah of Petra lived in the teeming Jewish Quarter of the city.

"I am looking for a friend who came to Alexandria several months ago. She is a singer and dancer, a very beautiful young woman named Leah of Petra," Onesimus said.

"A Jewess?"

"Part Jew and part Greek. She comes from Petra."

"There is no Jewess named Leah of Petra in the theater here, nor in the Jewish Quarter. I know the area well. But if you want to see dancing"—his eyes lit up—"you must let me take you to see Flamen perform. No one should visit Alexandria without seeing the most famous dancer in the Roman Empire."

# 19

A few days after their visit with Philo, a slave came to the house where Onesimus and Mark lived with an invitation for them to meet at Philo's house, and from there, they would go to the theater. It was mid-afternoon and people thronged the streets, dodging through a constant stream of chariots, carriages, and sedan chairs to cross the busiest intersection of the city.

Philo had to shout at several chairs before one large enough for three people stopped before them. Four slaves were chained to the carrying handles, lest they drop the chair and run away after receiving the price. A few men controlled almost the entire public-chair concession in the city and thus able to set the price at which they rented their conveyance to those who needed them. Richer Alexandrians, of course, had private chairs borne by their own slaves, but any man could be carried about the city in a style equaling his fortune merely by hailing a conveyance that was for hire.

Along the street of Canopus they were born swiftly through the Brucheion. Swarms of people were moving toward the waterfront, where much of the social life of the masses took place in the evening. When darkness fell, the courtesans would saunter from their quarters in the high-tiered buildings along the streets housing the teeming thousands of the Greek Quarter, while the sea breeze molded flimsy draperies to voluptuous bodies calculated with intent. There the gallants could write on the stone parapets with bits of charcoal their choice for an assignation, with the added forethought of the price to be paid. And seeing it, the lady chosen could hurry to the meeting or erase the offer contemptuously because the price was too low.

Through the Rhakotis, called the Greek Quarter, the chair moved slowly toward the Necropolis Gate, near where the smaller library of the museum was located close to the serapeum, the temple to the artificial god created by the Ptolemies to join the worship of Isis and Osiris. The streets of the Rhakotis were narrow, and they were stopped often by trains of mules bearing great bulbous wine skins and baskets of fruit to be sold that evening to the idlers thronging the waterfront.

In the center of the Greek Quarter was the open square of the market place, now almost depleted of provisions, for it was late afternoon. Here the stalls were loaded during the night, ready for the crowds that came shopping in the morning. But in the late afternoon, it was a wild place of tumbled bales and wrecks of baskets, where squashed fruits and vegetables made the stones of the pavement slippery. In the booths, sellers cried the remaining wares, a few green beans wilted from lying in the open all day, too ripe berries passed over by discerning shoppers earlier when the produce was fresh, roots of lotus, wilted lettuce, baskets of olives, and all the thousand and one foods necessary to satisfy the varied tastes of so many nationalities.

Near the market were many open-fronted eating places, where attendants had already begun setting out food to tempt the crowds beginning to throng the streets. Preserved figs and dates, flat cakes, some spiced, some plain, smoked fish and eel, all were temptingly displayed before the chattering crowd.

As they neared the theater, female voices shrieked from tier to tier of the high-fronted tenements and across the narrow streets, laughing, singing, or calling out a frank invitation to men passing on the streets below. But no matter how intently he listened to the voices of the city, nowhere did Onesimus hear the sound of a girl's voice as clear as the bell whose tones it resembled, or the twang of a giant cithara in the wild barbaric dances of the desert country.

It was said of the Alexandrians that they slept by day and roistered the whole night long and, looking about him tonight, Onesimus could well believe it. The weather was still warm, although winter was approaching, and the babbling of voices in every tongue of the world filled the air. On most every corner was a drinking house from which came shouts and coarse laughter, mingled with the happy squeals of the women who thronged there with the men.

It was on just such a warm evening as this, Onesimus remembered, that he had walked across the city of Rome to Demetrius's house with Leah and she had kissed him before going inside. Would he ever find her here in this teeming city? He wondered. If Leah had left Alexandria, someone among the mariners who sailed regularly to all the seaport cities of the empire might remember her and Demetrius, or at least the height and the hawk-like profile of the Nabatean, Hadja, but no such luck.

He stopped to speak to Phoenician traders, tall men with long hair and jutting beaks of noses, guarding piled-up bales of the rich purple fabric used for Roman uniforms, but learned nothing. He questioned sailors who traveled beyond the Pillars of Hercules to the land called Britannia, returning with vast stores of amber and crude tin, but to no avail. The quest seemed hopeless now, for he did not know where else to look for her.

The drama and dance were favorite diversions of the pleasure-loving Alexandrians, where the performances began in mid-afternoon and ran until darkness had fallen. A great crowd moved toward the massive stone walls of the great theater near the waterfront, a sight to be seen nowhere else in the world.

When he stepped out of the carriage, Onesimus stopped in astonishment. It was the first time he had come here at dusk, and he was not prepared for what he saw. A mirror reflected seaward the light of the great fires built nightly on the platform atop the Pharos, but the flames themselves were bright enough to light up the harbor and the great broad causeway leading across it to the island upon which the lighthouse stood.

"It is always like this when Flamen dances," Philo explained as they were pushing through the crowd. "The theater goers worship her. There has never been another like her in Alexandria."

"Is she a courtesan?" Onesimus knew that actresses belonged generally to this group.

Philo shrugged. "Some claim she is not. Men who have sought her favors and been repulsed will wager she is a virgin. Whatever she is, her power over men is greater than that of any other woman in Alexandria. She is rich already from gifts by wealthy men who seek her favors."

"Why do they seek her if she refuses them?"

Philo smiled. "You should know human nature well enough to realize that a man will beggar himself for a beautiful woman who denies him, when he would soon become tired of her if she yielded. Courtesan or not, this Flamen is smart and cold blooded. Just a month ago, Flavius, lost his position as tax collector because he stole tax moneys to buy gifts for her. The day he was found out, she turned to another, and richer, man."

Philo had purchased tickets entitling them to seats in the great auditorium. They found their seats only a short distance from the stage. The first several rows were reserved for the nobility and the very rich. Just over the openings where the crowd entered, two elaborate boxes called tribunalia were set apart for even more important dignitaries.

"One of the tribunalia is always taken by Flamen's current suitors," Phil explained. "You can see that she caters only to very rich men. Nobody else could afford such a seat night after night."

Onesimus looked about him curiously, for it was the first time he had ever been in a theater. Before the stage was a broad semicircular platform on which the chorus sang and danced and before which the musicians sat.

A great partition separated the audience from the stage proper, but soon after they found their seats, it was lowered into a grooved slot in the floor at the edge of the stage, revealing the stage with its painted backdrop.

The auditorium filled rapidly, and a steady roar of conversation filled the air. It was a brilliant scene, for the vast semicircular theater was a riot of color from the tunics of the men and the vivid draperies of the women who sat with them. Hawkers moved up and down the aisles selling sweetmeats and small skins of wine with which a thirsty viewer might refresh himself. People shouted gaily to each other across the rows, relaying the latest bawdy story or the newest juicy bit of scandal.

The musicians soon began to play the opening chorus, but there was little letup in the hum of conversation. Shortly a group of jugglers appeared, tossing swords deftly to each other and catching them by the handles with amazing dexterity. After them, a beautiful girl in jeweled breastplates and a golden girdle set a number of swords upon the floor and danced among them nimbly, missing the points, it seemed, by only a finger's breadth.

Next a troupe of girls in flimsy tunics ran out with garlands of flowers in their hair and carrying golden lyres in their hands. They sang a tender love song, then, putting the lyres on the edge of the raised stage above them, began to dance. All were very graceful and made a lovely picture in their flaming, revealing draperies.

After the dancing, the musicians began a strange haunting melody which Onesimus had never heard but which Philo said was a song of ancient Egypt, and a dark-skinned girl ran to the center of the stage and bowed, her extended fingertips touching the floor. When she raised, her writhing arms slowly and stood erect, Philo told Mark and Onesimus that her name was Albina.

"Next to Flamen, Albina is the best dancer they have," Philo observed. "A lovely girl as well."

The dark-skinned girl wore only a white silken cloth about her loins, but she was so lovely to look at that Onesimus could not think of her as being wanton in the display of her body. Her dance was strange to him, a thing of stylized postures with fingers together and hands extended in many odd positions, but the audience, especially the Egyptians, loved it, and Onesimus judged that it was a favorite of her people. When she finished, applause filled the theater and she came back once to bow to the audience.

On the performances went, for a regular program in the Alexandrian theater lasted four hours. Finally a group of black women from Africa danced the strange, sensuous tribal dances of their people, their naked bodies glistening with sweat in the light of an actual fire built in a great copper pot on the stage.

"Flamen will be coming soon," Philo said. "Her current suitor is in his box."

Onesimus looked across at the seat in the tribunalia which had until now been empty and saw that a tall man with a cold hard face had taken his place. The Roman was graying at the temples but very handsome.

"That is Plotinus," Philo explained. "I heard that he has already spent thousands of denarii on Flamen. He is one of the most important men in Alexandria."

"What does this Flamen do that makes her so popular in the theater?" Onesimus asked curiously. "She can hardly wear less clothing than the dancers who have gone before her."

"She wears more. They say when she first came to Alexandria, the director wanted her to dance naked like the others, but she refused. Wait until you see her, and you will understand the magic she uses upon a crowd, even when more fully clothed than many women in the audience tonight."

The last of the black dancers scurried from the stage and the massive curtain rose, creaking from the depths beneath it. It was already dark, and the attendants began to light torches on either side of the stage itself while a hush fell over the crowd in anticipation of the main attraction. Then, as slowly as it had risen, the curtain descended again and a scene of fairy-like beauty was revealed.

A flower garden had been wheeled upon the stage while the curtain was up. A bench stood in the garden beside the little fountain playing there as naturally as if it were real, and flowers were cunningly arranged so that they seemed to be growing around it. The sheer beauty of the scene brought a burst of spontaneous applause from the audience.

When the applause had died away, a woman appeared from the flower-decked arbor beside the bench, carrying a lyre in her hands. She was dressed in a clinging gown of dazzling white, girded about her waist and beneath her breasts with silvery ribbon, and on her flaming red hair, a circlet of jewels sparkled in the light of the torches beside the stage. Applause thundered throughout the building again, and she waited patiently for it to subside before plucking the strings of the lyre and beginning to sing. The song, when it reached Onesimus's ears, was familiar, as familiar as when he had first heard it one day on the streets leading into Rome.

# 20

Listening as she sang, drinking in her beauty with his eyes and his ears, Onesimus could see that Leah had changed somewhat in the months since she left Rome. It seemed to him that her body had grown more womanly and less girlish, but her voice had matured as well. Where before it had been beautiful, the tones were now richer and deeper, a voice to stir a man's pulse and set the blood pounding in their temples.

It was easy to see why she had captured the admiration of the jaded crowds of Alexandria, for looking around the theater, Onesimus saw not a woman who could even approach her in beauty and sheer personal allure, although the most famous courtesans of all Egypt were here tonight. Plotinus was leaning forward in his box, and as she finished her song, Onesimus saw Leah glance up to the tribunalia where he sat and smile, before bowing to the thunderous applause of the audience.

"Is she not lovely?" Philo asked.

"Even more that she was when she was in Rome," Onesimus said without taking his eyes from the white figure on the stage below.

Philo's eyes widened. "Do you mean—"

"The woman called Flamen in Alexandria is Leah of Petra, the girl I have been seeking."

The lawyer's eyes popped. "Then why could you not find her?"

"She no longer uses her name. And she seems not to have let it be known here that she is a Jew."

Philo nodded. "She was wise. We Jews are not loved, even in Alexandria, where we outnumber almost everyone else. And no Roman would marry her if he knew she was Jewish."

"She is only half Jew," Onesimus explained. "She was brought up as a Greek."

"Flamen," Philo mused. "The Torch. She could hardly have chosen a more appropriate name under which to dance. Sometimes she does resemble a burning brand."

"A Nabatean musician named Hadja gave her the name," Onesimus explained. "He always called her the living flame. She would naturally take the name Flamen as an actress. I was stupid not to think of it before."

When the tumult subsided, the music began another melody, a wailing, sensuous beat. Now Leah's body was the promise of woman's eternal lure for men. Under its spell, the very sound of breathing from the vast audience seemed to deepen with desire, for the lure of all the delights in a pagan paradise was in her body. "I have seen naked women from the east dance many times," Philo said hoarsely. "But the clothing that Flamen wears makes her ten times more desirable."

Onesimus glanced up at the box of the tribunalia, Plotinus was leaning forward, his eyes fixed upon the seductive undulating figure on the stage. The Roman's face was pale, and sweat stood out on his forehead. In a sudden moment of insight into the man's thoughts, Onesimus knew that Plotinus had not yet possessed Leah of Petra. A man could not desire with such overwhelming intensity a fruit he had already tasted. The thought, however, brought him little joy.

"How can you be so calm, Onesimus?" Philo asked hoarsely. "You love the girl. Are you not consumed by desire for her as is Plotinus up there?"

Slowly Onesimus shook his head. "Flamen is more beautiful than Leah of Petra ever was," he admitted. "But the woman dancing there is not the same. An evil spirit has laid hold of her."

"It is an evil spirit every man here save yourself would give his soul to possess then. No wonder she can do anything she wishes with men."

The dance came to its inevitable climax, and the lovely flame-haired figure on the stage slowly sank to the floor with her arms outstretched before her while the crowd broke into a great thunder of applause. Men leaped to their feet and threw empty wine skins and the dried leaves in which sweetmeats had been wrapped into the air, shouting their approval as Leah ran from the stage. But the crowd shouted again and again for her, and she was forced to return several times before they would let her go. Finally when the great curtain began to rise slowly from its slot in the floor, Onesimus stood up. "I want to speak to her," he said. "Do you know how to get behind the scenes?"

"Of course. Albina sometimes dines with me after a performance."

Behind the great stage, everything seemed to be confusion as they sought Flamen's dressing room. Scantily clad women hurried past, scenery was being moved, for there would be another performance tomorrow, and musicians were leaving the theater with their instruments under their arms. At the entrance to a short corridor leading to the dressing room of the principal dancer a picture of a torch had been painted on the wall. Beneath it stood a Roman soldier in polished harness with Plotinus personal crest upon his helmet below the eagles of Rome. He had a drawn sword in his hand and as they approached, he held the blade across the passage, barring them from approaching.

"I would speak to the dancer Flamen," Onesimus said courteously. "We are old friends from Rome."

"No one visits Flamen except by permission of Plotinus," the soldier snapped, as if this happened all the time. "On your way."

"But—but—"

"Did you hear the guard, Jew?" a harsh voice asked behind him. Onesimus turned to see Plotinus standing only a yard away. At close rang, the face of Plotinus was even colder and more foreboding than it had been from the box.

"I heard him," Onesimus said in a courteous tone. "If you would send word to Flamen that Onesimus of Perga is here to see her, I am sure she would admit me. We are friends from Rome."

"Flamen would never have a Jew as a friend," Plotinus said contemptuously. "I know this fellow Philo is a leader of the Jews."

"I tell you, Flamen and I are friends."

"Silence, Jewish dog!" Plotinus snapped, reddening with anger. He was wearing a mailed glove, and a sudden murderous light flared in the cold eyes. It did not for the moment occur to Onesimus that Plotinus would strike him, so he was totally unprepared for the smash of the mailed fist against his temple. There was a sudden sharp pain as the metal cut through yielding skin, then darkness engulfed him.

At first, Onesimus thought he was back in his own quarters, where he lived with Mark. It was night, for an oil lamp burned in a bracket on the wall and the room was just like that in which he lived, one of thousands of such rooms in the many-storied tenements making up the Greek Quarter. And yet something was different about this one, the colorful cushions of the couch on which he lay, and the faint perfume in the air.

Something moved in the far corner, and he made out a graceful feminine figure in a white silken robe. For one thrilling moment, he thought it was Leah, but as the girl came into the circle of light, he recognized the dark skin and clearly etched features of Albina, the Egyptian dancer.

"Have you decided to wake up?" Albina's fingers touched his forehead, and he realized that a bandage partially covered his head.

Now he began to remember what had happened.

"Was I unconscious long?" he asked Albina.

"Almost six hours by the water clock. I saw Plotinus strike you in the corridor leading to Flamen's dressing room, and your friend Mark and Philo brought you here while you were unconscious. We thought best for you to stay here."

"But it is night." He started to push himself up on his elbows, but the room began to reel. Albina stooped quickly and put her arm about his shoulders, lowering him gently back to the cushions. "It is almost morning," she said, "but what difference does that make?"

"Have we spent the night here alone?"

"Most of it." She smiled. "I do not mind. Why should you?"

"But your reputation?"

She shrugged. "I'm a dancer in the theater. Everybody thinks we are courtesans, whether we are or not, so we soon stop worrying about what they think. You must lie still now."

"Did Le—Flamen know I was looking for her?" he asked.

Albina shook her head. "Plotinus is insanely jealous. He posts a guard before her dressing room when she comes to the theater, and no man can enter it, not even the director. You should not have tried to see her at the theater, Onesimus. Plotinus might have killed you if Philo and Mark had not taken you away to my place. He can do almost anything he likes here in Alexandria. They say the governor obeys his orders."

"But I have been seeking her for weeks," Onesimus protested.

"I am one of the few who knows that Flamen has Jewish blood," Albina explained. "We were very close when she first came to Alexandria. I was the principal dancer then, and she was one of the chorus, but she soon stood above me."

"Most people would hate her for it."

The dancer shook her head. "Flamen is a great artist, the greatest I have ever known. No one could hate her for the gift the gods have given her. But she has no soul."

"Why do you say that?"

"Women were meant to fill a great need of man, Onesimus. In her arms, he can find release from the cares of the day, and she can give him strong sons and daughters so that his line may not die. But a woman who stirs up men's passions, not to satisfy them but to deliberately use them for her own gain, is dishonest."

"Then it is true that she does not give herself to these men who follow after her?"

A look of pain and disappointment came into her beautiful dark eyes. "You love her, too, don't you, Onesimus?" she said softly.

"I have loved her from the time we first met," he explained, "but not as the woman who danced tonight. She was an innocent girl then, lovely and unspoiled. Now..." He did not finish the sentence. The thought of what Leah had become brought pain.

"It is hard to believe that Flamen was ever like that," Albina said. "But you love her, Onesimus, so I will tell you what I believe—that Flamen has been mistress to nothing but her own greed for gold and power."

"It is not greed that drives her," Onesimus said, "but the desire for revenge."

"What need for revenge could be that strong?"

"She was cruelly ravished by a man, a Roman named Domitian," he explained. "She followed him to Alexandria several months ago. She wants to kill him."

"I have been told that Domitian has been in the desert east of Alexandria training soldiers. Philo knows everything that goes on in Alexandria, and he said these soldiers that Domitian is training will soon march on Jerusalem with his older brother Titus in command of those troops."

"Then Domitian will be back in Alexandria soon?"

"Only for a few days," she informed him. "Philo says the emperor has called him back to Rome."

Hope rose in the heart of Onesimus. When Domitian leaves Alexandria, he thought, perhaps Leah would give up this idea of revenge and go back to Rome with him.

"I can understand why she hates all Romans, especially Domitian. Any woman would. And yet you continue to love her even through that, Onesimus? You must be a saint."

Onesimus shook his head as Albina smoothed the bandage upon his head with gentle fingers. "I have never known a man like you, Onesimus. If Flamen treats you as she does the others,"— she took a deep breath—"why do I find it so hard to tell you that I would be happy to bear you strong children? And to comfort you in my arms against the troubles of the world? I am a dancer and the people believe me a prostitute, but I have lain with no man for his gold, or ever will. Still no good man would want to marry me because of this."

"I think you are wrong." He put his hand over hers. "Many men would want you for what your are, not what people think you to be."

"Men like you might, Onesimus," she agreed. "But I have seen no other one. I would save you the sorrow I know Flamen will bring you, but if you must see her, I will tell you where she may be found. She dwells on the shore of Lake Mareotis outside the wall of the city, where many of the rich have villas. I am told that the house belongs to Plotinus, and he keeps soldiers always on guard there, but if you walk along the shore, you can enter the garden between the water and the walls."

"How do you know this?" he asked.

Albina smiled. "Philo tells me everything, but be careful that you are not taken for a thief when you go to see Flamen. The guards would make short work of you."

# 21

Onesimus suffered no ill effects from his wound by the mailed fist of Plotinus. In a few days, the slight headache which followed it was gone, and the cut in his scalp was healing so that he no longer needed a bandage. Late one afternoon, he set off for the villa where Albina had told him Leah lived. Darkness was already falling when he reached the line of elaborate villas on the shore of Lake Mareotis.

The shores of the large inland body of water formed by the mouth of the Nile were very fertile. Fruit gardens and vineyards flourished and grew everywhere, for there was not a day in the year that something did not bloom in Alexandria. Some of the streets led down to the water itself, where boat landings had been placed to facilitate traffic back and forth between the city and the luxurious gardens on the eight islands outlined in the early dusk against the reddish tint of the sky from the setting sun.

From the canal, a regular line of ferry boats crossed the lake to the islands and on to the mainland beyond. Across the water moved an endless procession of grain barges bringing corn for Rome and Alexandria from the rich delta in the interior. Small galleys, graceful pleasure boats with colorful sails, and light skiffs scurried about seeking to reach their moorings before darkness fell completely.

A soft breeze flowed down the Nile Valley toward its mouth, bathing the city in a pleasant warmth and wafting over it a fragrant aroma from the flowers and spice groves on the lake shore. Tonight a great crowd would be promenading along the waterfront, but here on the lake shore, there was peace and quiet.

True to what Albina told him, two Roman soldiers guarded the door to Flamen's villa, identified by the same picture of a torch that marked her dressing room. Onesimus knew better than to approach them after his painful experience in the theater. Instead he walked along the street before the waterfront homes and counted the villas until he came to a path running down to the water. Returning then near the water's edge along the shore in the dusk, he had no difficulty in locating Leah's home.

Pines, maples, and spice trees grew down to the water's edge, where a flock of ducks, disturbed by his passing, rose into the air with a whirring of wings, and as he turned along a path leading through the luxurious garden that grew between the villa identified by the torch and the lake itself, a group of flamingos starred at him haughtily before moving aside for him to pass.

Onesimus considered whether he should announce his presence in some way but decided not to do so, hoping to surprise Leah and Demetrius. As he moved closer to the house along a winding gravel walk, a shadow suddenly darted from behind a tree and a brawny arm encircled his neck, bringing him up, choking, on his toes. "What do you seek in the garden of Flamen besides death, stranger?" a deep voice inquired. The voice sounded familiar.

"Hadja!" Onesimus croaked, for the Nabatean's massive arm was pressing on his windpipe. "It is I, Onesimus."

The pressure was released suddenly. "Praise be to Ahura-Mazda!" Hadja cried, embracing Onesimus and threatening to crush his bones again. "Why do you come through the garden like a thief?"

"I was knocked down by a Roman when I tried to see Leah at the theater a few days ago," Onesimus explained.

"It was Plotinus?" Hadja growled. "Someday I will slip a knife between his ribs! You have seen the living flame?"

"In the theater only."

"What did you think of her?"

"She has changed, Hadja, but she is more beautiful than ever."

"It is the beauty of evil. Sometimes I think as many as seven devils have possessed her," the Nabatean growled.

"Is she happy, Hadja? If she is, perhaps I should go away."

The musician shook his head. "She lives only to bring Romans to ruin. But come and see Demetrius. He will be glad to see you, Onesimus."

Hadja led Onesimus to a room at the back of the house. The villa was sumptuously furnished; beautiful paintings and expensive statues were everywhere, and deep rugs covered the floor. "The living flame is not here," Hadja explained, "but she will be home from the theater soon."

Only a small oil lamp burned in the chamber where Demetrius lay propped up on a couch, and the curtains were drawn so that the room was almost dark. Hadja ushered Onesimus in and shut the door leaving the two of them alone.

"I heard someone enter," the old man quavered. "Who is it?"

"An old friend from Rome," Onesimus told him gently.

"From Rome? Onesimus!" he cried. "I recognized the voice."

Onesimus embraced his old friend. "I knew you would come," the lyre maker cried. "You find us in a sad state, my friend. This cursed desire for revenge has made another person of Leah. She thinks of nothing but making money and gaining power over Romans. It was an evil day when we left Rome."

"Tell me about yourself," Onesimus urged.

"What is there to tell," Demetrius sighed. "I have all I want to eat and wine to drink, but what good is that when I have no appetite and my health is so bad. It is hard for me to breath with so much pressure on my lungs. But enough about me. Have you seen Leah?"

"At the theater. But when I sought to speak to her, a Roman forbade me."

"Plotinus!" Demetrius spat out the word as Hadja had done. "If she would only hurry with the job of getting his money and ruining him. The others were stupid, but Plotinus is dangerous."

"Have there been others?" Until now he had hoped all the things he had heard might not be true.

"A procession of simpletons who beggared themselves, hoping she would lie with them."

"What of Domitian? Has Leah seen him?"

"No, they say he has been in the desert training soldiers, but I can't help fearing for Leah when he does come back to Alexandria. How long can you hate without your very hate consuming you?"

"I don't know. I never hated anyone very long."

"I know," Demetrius agreed. "You are a good man. God knows there are few enough of them in Alexandria."

A slave came in bringing two trays of food. While Onesimus ate, the slave fed Demetrius, but the old lyre maker had lost his appetite, something that could have never happened in the old days! His enjoyment of food and wine then had been limited only by the lack of them. He pushed away the silver goblet when it was still half filled. "Take the food away, child," he told the slave. "I have no appetite anymore."

Onesimus stood up. "I had better go now. Leah may be coming soon."

"But you are an old friend," Demetrius protested. "Why should you not be welcome in this house?"

"I did not tell you the whole of my experience with Plotinus the other day," Onesimus explained. "He knocked me unconscious. I have no desire for a second dose."

Demetrius cursed savagely. Neither of them heard the door open or realized they were not alone until Leah cried from the door, "What are you cursing about, Demetrius? You sound more like yourself than you have in months." In the darkness, she had not noticed that the lyre maker had a visitor. The night was hot, and when she came from the theater, she had put on a robe of bombyx that Roman women often wore in their bedrooms. Knowing that Demetrius could not see well, she had not hesitated to come into the room in such a state of undress, with the sweet lines of her body almost fully revealed by the gauzy fabric as she stood in the doorway. Suddenly Leah realized who was there with Demetrius. "Onesimus!" she cried, and her face flushed as she tried to gather the inadequate robe about her body. "You— Excuse me," she stammered, and was gone.

"What was the matter with her?" Demetrius demanded.

"She wasn't exactly dressed."

"That's the only sensible habit she has picked up from the Romans." Demetrius chuckled. "Their women go practically naked in hot weather, and it certainly makes life more interesting, even for an old sot like me."

Leah came back a moment later, wrapped in a long robe, and gave Onesimus her hand. "Why didn't you let me know you had come to Alexandria?" she said.

"He has been here for several weeks," Demetrius growled. "But could not find us because you have taken another name. And when he did, the guards would not let him see you. How long are you going to keep up this insane life, Leah?"

"We agreed not to talk about that, Demetrius," she said sharply. "Remember?"

"It is your life," he grunted. "Ruin it if you must."

Leah took a taper from its bracket on the wall and held it so she could see Onesimus. "You have not changed," she said softly. "You will always be the same."

"I wish I could say as much about you, Leah."

For an instant, there was a look of pain in her eyes, then she laughed, a brittle sound that was oddly like a sob. In an instant, she was no longer the Leah he loved. "Of course I have changed," she said somewhat sharply. "When I left Rome, I was only a slip of a girl. I am a woman now."

"You are a beautiful woman, Leah, even more than you were in Rome. You have come a long way in a short time. I saw you dance a few days ago," he told her. "And you deserve to have Alexandria at your feet. Are you happy with what you have accomplished, Leah?"

Again the look of pain showed momentarily in her eyes before she gave a brittle laugh. "I am rich. The leading men of Alexandria are at my feet, and the people adore me," she cried airily. "What else could a woman want?"

"The love of a good man instead of the lust of these accursed Romans," Demetrius growled. "It was an evil day when you left Rome."

"How did you get into the villa?" Leah asked, as she ignored Demetrius and led Onesimus out into the garden.

"By the shore. After my experience with Plotinus the other day, I did not risk the guards."

"He told me he had knocked down a tradesman who was trying to see me. Of course I had no way of knowing it was you."

"Would you have acknowledged me if you had?" he asked deliberately.

"Onesimus!" she cried. "How could you say that?"

"You left Rome without saying good-bye to me. And apparently you have denied your Jewish blood…"

"I have not. I merely kept it a secret."

"But why if you are not ashamed of it?"

She put her hand on his arm. "You must try to understand, Onesimus. As a Jewish, I would have had little chance to succeed here in the theater. You know how the Romans hate Jews, and after all, I am part Greek."

"Have you also forgotten the God of your people?"

She laughed again, the same brittle note. "Why should I be concerned with the Most High? He would have let me be sold into slavery if Simon and Demetrius had not saved me, and He forsook me when I needed help that horrible night in Rome."

"You are rich and famous, but no one is happy with what you are doing, not even you."

"I am doing what I want to do," she said simply. "What I have sworn to do."

"And if what you have sworn to do is evil."

"The evil will be on my soul. Why concern yourself with it?" She put her hand on his arm appealingly. "Please, let us not quarrel, Onesimus, when we haven't seen each other for so many months. Why did you come to Alexandria?"

"I came because I love you, Leah, to learn whether you still love me."

For a moment she did not speak, and he thought there were tears in her eyes. "And now that you know," she asked almost in a whisper, "why don't you leave?"

"But I don't know. You haven't told me yourself."

"You must not love me, Onesimus," she said pleadingly. "It can only mean unhappiness to you. Go back to Rome and forget you ever knew Leah of Petra."

He took her in his arms, turning her until she faced him there in the darkness of the garden. "When you swear by the Most High that you no longer love me, Leah, I will go," he said. "It is the only thing that will send me away."

He heard the sob in her throat, and then her arms were about him and she was clinging to him, her face buried against his chest, sobbing unrestrained. Wisely he held her thus until she was quiet, then her took her chin in his hand and, lifting it, kissed her gently upon her lips. The salt of her tears was upon them, and she clung to him with her mouth soft and yielding beneath his own for a long moment before she pushed him away. Then she dried her eyes with the flowing sleeve of her robe and pushed the soft hair back from her face. "It has been a long time since I have wept like that, Onesimus," she said. "Nothing helps a woman more when she is troubled."

"You need be troubled no longer," he said. "Come back to Rome with me as my wife."

"You should know by now that I am not like other women, Onesimus. I would not come to you as your wife when a part of me lived only to hate Domitian. I could never be dishonest with you. I love you too much for that." But when he would have taken her in his arms again, she put her hands on his chest in a restraining gesture. "Do you think I want to see Hadja and Demetrius—yes, even you unhappy? But until I carry out my oath to kill Domitian, I can never be the girl you loved back in Rome."

"Hadja was right then. A demon has possessed you."

"Hadja claims there are seven." She smiled. "Perhaps he is right. But the demon of hate will possess my soul until I kill the man who put it there."

"Have you seen Domitian since you left Rome?"

"No." She hesitated, then continued. "Plotinus is close to the emperor, though. He has told me that the emperor has called him back to Rome, so I expect him back in Alexandria soon. I understand he has been in the desert east of Alexandria training troops. If I don't get the job done here, I will get it done back in Rome," she stated dogmatically.

"Did you tell Plotinus you want to see Domitian?"

"I only told him I hate Domitian and want to humiliate him. Plotinus is cruel himself, so he understands and sympathizes with that sort of motive."

"Then you're using Plotinus this way is only part of your plan of revenge?"

"Of course," she said. "Do you think I could love a Roman after what Domitian did to me? They give me gold because they think I will give myself to them in return. But when I get their money, I throw them aside."

"When will you be through with Plotinus?"

"When Domitian comes back to Alexandria."

"Give up this madness, Leah," he begged. "You can't murder a man that easily."

"It will be difficult," she admitted coolly, "but I will do it. My plans are made, and all Rome will know the hour of my vengeance."

Onesimus thought she was only deluding herself, and yet he could see no way to make this clear to her.

A sharp challenge came suddenly from the guard in front of the villa. "Go," Leah whispered. "And stay by the shore. Plontinus has come to take me to a dinner this evening. I will tell him later that you are a physician treating Demetrius." She stood on her toes and kissed him quickly. "Leave Alexandria. Believe me, it is best for both of us."

She was gone in a rustle of silk, leaving Onesimus alone in the darkness. As he made his way through the garden to the shore and past the wall that ran to the very water's edge, he saw lamps being lit in the villa and heard the gay laugh of the woman called Flamen as she greeted her Roman admirer.

Seeing Leah once again, Onesimus knew that his love for her burned now with an ever deeper fire than it had in Rome. And since she had admitted that she loved him still, he knew he must prevent her somehow from carrying out this insane scheme to kill Domitian.

# 22

Knowing that he could do nothing to turn Leah away from her firm resolution to be revenged upon Domitian, Onesimus was tempted to do what she had advised, leave Alexandria and return to Rome.

Demetrius was able to leave the house on occasion, and then he moved with difficulty because of a plethora and dropsy that caused his body to swell. But when the old Greek musician was able to be up long enough, Onesimus took him to the theater to see Leah dance. Leah seemed to be inspired that night; never had Onesimus seen her dance more spiritedly or with more grace. And watching her beauty, the slender loveliness of her body as she moved about the stage in the expressive rhythm of the dance, he felt a deep sense of depression and foreboding grip his soul. She had embarked upon an insane course, he was sure, and yet he could do nothing at all to stop her. And his depression deepened when he glanced at the box usually reserved for the Roman governor of the city and saw Domitian sitting there, as handsome as a Greek god.

When the performance was ended, they made their way to Leah's dressing room through the corridors beneath the theater.

She anticipated their coming and left word for the guard to let them in. She still wore the costume in which she danced and was sitting before her dressing table when they entered, while her maid, a dark-skinned slave from Cyrene, brushed her hair. Leah got up and ran to kiss the old musician. "I was dancing for you, Demetrius," she cried. "Did you like it?"

"There has never been one to equal you, child." Demetrius's voice was thick with emotion. "This is the crowning moment of my life."

"We will have other moments," she promised gaily, "many of them."

"You have everything you wish for."

"Not everything," Leah said, suddenly serious, "but I am very near." She turned to Onesimus. "You saw him?"

"Yes. How long has he been in Alexandria?"

"He arrived today. I am told he sails for Rome tomorrow."

Onesimus shrugged. "We had better go, Demetrius," he said. "Doubtless the lady called Flamen will have suitors wishing to visit her."

Leah flushed at his tone, but before she could say anything a sharp-voiced challenge came from the guard outside the door. A moment later, the curtains were thrust arrogantly aside, revealing a tall man in the uniform of a Roman tribune. It was Domitian.

For a moment, Leah was like a marble statue, then as the young Roman strode forward and lifted her hand to his lips, color came into her cheeks and she relaxed. "I could not wait to meet you," Domitian said, kissing her hand. "Such beauty and talent deserve a more spontaneous tribute." And then, as his eyes met hers, a puzzled look came into his face. "Your face seems familiar."

"Does it?" Leah asked, still smiling, but her eyes were hard and cold.

Domitian seemed to realize for the first time that there were others in the room. He turned to them, and his eyes widened in surprise.

"I am Onesimus," he said quietly.

"And my name is Demetrius," the old musician added, "a lyre maker of Rome, lately come to Alexandria."

Domitian looked from them to Leah, and his eyes widened with amazement. "But you couldn't be the little dancer," he cried. "The one I knew in Rome."

Leah's voice cut him short. "In Alexandria, I am called Flamen," she said proudly.

"Leah of Petra," Domitian said softly. "You have come a long way, my dear. And you are more beautiful than ever. No wonder they tell me the men of Alexandria are at your feet."

"And you?" Leah added. Her voice was soft, almost coaxing. Hearing it, Onesimus could understand her power over men.

The tribune smiled. "No doubt I shall be there too," he said softly. "But it shall be from afar, unless you come back to Rome. I leave for Rome tomorrow."

Onesimus could stand it no more. "Come, Demetrius," he said, "I will take you home."

The Roman was hardly outside the room when Demetrius burst out, "The arrogant swine! And you!" He turned to Leah savagely. "Simpering and leading him on like a common prostitute. Have you forgotten what he did to you?"

The color slowly drained from Leah's cheeks, and her fingers clenched into the palms of her hands, leaving them dead white. "I have not forgotten," she said slowly, almost as if she were praying. "Before the Most High, I have not forgotten."

# PART IV

# ROME
## THE ARENA MIRACLE

# 23

With Nero back in Rome, the Christian community braced for the worst. Also returning to Rome from Alexandria was Nero's favorite tribune, Domitian. Leah, in order to carry out her revenge, would also leave Alexandria. It would take a couple of days to get everything in order, but she was determined to follow Domitian to Rome.

Her gold and expensive gifts would be secured in a strong box. Her clothes packed and ready, she informed Demetrius and the musicians, sending Hadja to tell Onesimus of her plans to leave. Mark told Onesimus that he would be staying in Alexandria to pastor the church that he had organized. Onesimus would go with Leah.

She bribed the two soldiers that Plotinus had guarding the front door of his villa. Leaving Plotinus villa that Leah had been living in, they boarded a ship early one morning and sailed to Rome.

Word was soon noised abroad that Flamen had left Alexandria and was on her way to Rome. This news was not missed by Domitian. At Puteoli, they rented a carriage for Demetrius, Leah, and the strong box. Onesimus and the others would walk along side. Finally they reached Rome, but her fame preceded her. As they entered Rome, a large crowd of people followed them, for word had spread that Flamen, the living flame, was back in Rome.

The crowd finally disbursed when they reached the home of Aquila and Priscilla. While Leah visited with them, Onesimus and the musicians made ready the house of Demetrius and unpacked the cart.

With Leah now home and resting from the long journey, Onesimus visited Paul and Luke, bringing them up to date on his stay in Alexandria, and Mark's desire to remain and pastor the church there.

A few days later, Nero sent out a proclamation announcing a gala event to celebrate the rebuilding of the old central part of Rome that had been destroyed by fire. There would also be a dinner prior to the celebration in honor of Domitian for his successful mission in Alexandria. A personal invitation came to Leah requesting Flamen to sing and dance at this dinner to be held in the emperor's palace.

With the colosseum still under construction, the event would be held in the amphitheater with a great cast of entertainers promised. Onesimus learned that Leah had received a personal invitation from the emperor to sing and dance at a dinner honoring Domitian. He suspected the invitation was Domitian's idea.

When Onesimus reached the house of Demetrius, Leah was away practicing with her musicians. If he had not loved her as he did, Onesimus would have been tempted to leave Rome and return to Colosse rather than stay and witness the inevitable ending of the tragic course of revenge upon which she was determined. But loving her, he could not desert her at a time when she might need him most.

And then there was Demetrius. The lyre maker was growing weaker, his body more and more swollen and distorted by the plethra and dropsy, which had grown much worse. When the accumulating fluid threatened to drown Demetrius in the secretions of his own body, Luke had dared to insert quills into the tremendous distended body to let it out, but they both knew this was but a temporary measure. His death would devastate Leah, and he needed to be there for her.

Demetrius lay propped up in bed. "Do you know any more about Leah's plan for revenge against Domitian?" Demetrius asked Onesimus.

"No. But she said once that all Rome will know the hour of her revenge."

"Then she must plan to kill him publicly. And the most dramatic way of achieving revenge would naturally appeal to her. But when would all Rome know the hour?...By Diana!" he cried. "She told me she was invited to sing at a dinner Nero was giving in honor of Domitian for his work in Alexandria. The dinner is planned the night before the festival is to begin."

"Do you suppose...?"

"Yes, I believe that is when she will try to kill Domitian," Demetrius said heavily.

"I have laid a heavy burden upon you, Onesimus." Demetrius put his hand upon the younger man's shoulder. "But I shall not live much longer, and I would like to be certain that someone I trust will be looking after Leah when I'm dead."

"But Demetrius—"

"Please, Onesimus. In a way, I welcome death, and I need only two things now to be able to die in peace. One is your promise that you will take care of Leah, and the other to know that you two will be married as soon as this business is over."

"You have my promise," Onesimus assured him.

Leah came in a few minutes later.

"Leah, I'm glad you are here. I want to talk to you and Onesimus together about something very important," Demetrius said. "Come sit here with Onesimus beside the bed."

She kissed Onesimus and sat down. Gently the old man caressed Leah's shining hair. "I have known for some time, dear," he said, "that I have only a little longer to live."

"No, Demetrius!" she cried, and clung to him. "Don't say it."

"I am in no pain," the old musician continued. "And I am not afraid to die, now that I know someone will look after you when I am gone."

She raised her head from his breast. "W-what do you mean?"

"Onesimus has promised me that he will watch over you."

"But he must not!" she cried, and turned to Onesimus. "Why should you be killed for me?"

"Do you expect to die after you have carried out your plan of revenge upon the Roman?" Demetrius asked.

"I know what I'm doing."

"We know too," Demetrius told her.

She looked startled. "But I have not told you."

"You are planning to kill Domitian during the dinner Nero is giving to honor Domitian."

"I will tell you nothing," she said quickly, and looked away, but not before they had seen from her expression that their guess was correct.

"This is my responsibility alone," she added grimly.

"But I had already planned to help you escape before Demetrius asked me."

"But why should you endanger your life for me, Onesimus?"

"Because I love you," he stated.

Her eyes filled with tears. "Dear sweet, Onesimus," she said softly, and for a moment she was the girl he had been afraid had ceased to exist. "I think my love for you is the only thing left in my heart by this demon of hatred. But you must have no part in this," she added firmly.

"You cannot keep me from standing by in case you need help."

"What could you do? The might of Rome will be against me."

"With God's help, anything is possible."

"Would you give up your life for me?" she asked softly.

"Have you forgotten the pledge of Ruth?" he asked. "It was given in love as a guide for all those who love each other.

"'Entreat me not to leave thee,'" she repeated softly, "'or to return from following after thee; for wither thou goest I will go; and where thou lodgest, I will lodge: thy people shall be my people, and thy God my God: where thou diest I will die, and there will I be buried: the Lord do so to me, and more also, if aught but death part me and thee.'" And suddenly she burst into tears and ran from the room.

Demetrius died quietly in his sleep and was buried with his beloved cithara in his hands as he requested in the catacombs. As she and Onesimus walked home from the catacombs, Leah looked up at the praetorium as they were passing and shivered as if with dread. "I hope you never know what it is to have hatred in your soul, Onesimus," she said. "It is like a disease, eating away at everything that is good in you."

"You must do what your heart tells you to do. No one can do more. But be sure you are listening to your heart and not a demon of hate."

"Then I must go through with it," she said firmly.

"And you still refuse to tell me how you are going to carry out your plans?"

She nodded. "If you have no part in my guilt, Onesimus, then you will have no part in my fate, whatever it shall be."

# 24

The evening of Nero's dinner, Onesimus had borrowed Luke's mule and cart for Leah to ride in, as he and the musicians walked along side. Leaving the mule and cart at the praetorium, they walked up the hill to the emperor's palace. At the entrance, two guards were there and allowed Leah and her musicians to enter. Onesimus was not invited in. He anticipated this and walked back down the hill and circled around to the side door of the banqueting hall. It was getting dark, and he thanked God no guards attended the side entrance, and there in seclusion he waited.

Most of Nero's guests had already arrived and were seated for dinner with much wine being consumed. Leah and her musicians were seated at a separate table against a wall near the alcove where the musicians would play, and where she would dance.

Soon Nero, dressed in his royal trappings stood and welcomed his guests. There were high-ranking officials of the emperor's court, senators and others. Then he introduced Domitian and spoke of his accomplishments in Alexandria. He had organized and trained an elite force of Roman soldiers that would soon lay siege on Jerusalem, with his older brother Titus as commander leading this mission.

After dinner was served, Leah's musicians assembled in the alcove. Then with the crash of cymbals, the music began. A shout of approval rose from the crowd as Leah stood erect. She seemed in truth a goddess of love and beauty with her coppery hair, bound only by a white circlet, the regal lines of the white gown she wore emphasizing the loveliness of her divine body.

Domitian whispered to Nero. "There has never been such a beautiful woman. She is a bride indeed fit for a god."

Before Leah began to dance, she bowed to Nero, and then purposely to Domitian. Domitian, evidently flattered at being the center of attention, bowed and smiled back at Leah. Listening at the side door, Onesimus wondered if she would be able to go through with what she planned and found himself praying that she would come to her senses and give up at the last moment. Yet, remembering how the past several months had been a preparation for this moment of triumph over the man who had treated her so cruelly, he hardly dared hope that reason would prevail over the almost insane obsession that guided Leah now.

Leah poised with her arms uplifted, as the music seemed to caress her body, creating in its beauty a fluid rhythm in cadence with the throbbing beat of the scabella and the strings, and wail of the flute. Slowly at first, then faster as the rhythm quickened, she began to move in a provocative dance that set the onlookers to breathing hard with the grip of its allure.

As she danced, the circlet about her head came loose and was tossed aside, letting the glorious mass of her hair stream about her shoulders, enveloping them in a cascade of coppery gold. She was like a spinning torch, and a roar of spontaneous applause came from the audience. Naked lust was in the Romans' eyes.

In the midst of her dancing, she whirled before the tall tribune, her eyes mocking him. Faster the rhythm went as she moved about the open circle of the crowd, skillfully eluding those who tried to touch her. The music rose to its climax, then ceased upon a crash of the cymbals. Standing on her toes, her lovely breasts rising and falling rapidly with the excitement and effort of her dancing, Leah poised like a statue of Aphrodite herself, eyes shining, while the crowd deepened the thunder of its applause and shouts of approval.

While the applause continued, Leah walked back to Hadja and with her back to the crowd, slipped his long knife into the folds of her dress and walked deliberately back to where Domitian stood.

As she stood before him, he leaned over and whispered in her ear. "I have known many women, but none more beautiful than you. I have thought about you often," as he fondled a lock of her hair hanging over her breast. "My carriage can take us to my villa immediately. Would you like that?"

Leah's heart beat rapidly as she screamed, "You bastard!" and with all her strength, quickly shoved the long blade into his stomach.

Domitian's eyes widened in horror as he dropped to his knees holding the handle of the blade in his hand, with blood streaming down his white tunic. "Help me!" he screamed. "I'm dying!" Nero and his guest stood with mouths open in shock.

Leah turned as Hadja grasped her hand and ran toward the hallway leading to the side entrance of the banquet room.

Onesimus had heard the commotion inside and opened the door to enter just as Hadja and Leah rushed out. "Run, run to the catacombs," he shouted, hoping he could delay any pursuit which might give them time to escape. As he entered the hallway, he met two praetorian guards which he quickly dispatched with his mighty fists. Moving on down the hallway, he met three more guards. Kicking the sword out of the hand of the guard nearest him, he grabbed him and lifted him above his head and threw him against the other two, knocking them down. He hesitated for a second, wondering what he would face next, when a blow to the back of his head knocked him to his knees. Stunned, the next blow knocked him unconscious. One of the two guards he had met first recovered enough to pick up a small bronze statue from its pedestal, and hit him in the back of his head.

Onesimus awakened with a throbbing headache. There was caked blood on the back of his head. It was dark, except for a torch he saw burning some distance away. There were iron bars between him and the light. The last thing he remembered was fighting the praetorian guards. Then his thoughts turned to Leah. Did she and Hadja make it to the catacombs?

As his vision cleared, he saw that there were other cells like his own. Soon a guard of the prison came to his cell and offered him a jug of water. "You are in deep trouble, big guy," he stated.

"Where am I?"

"You are in the praetorian prison, and I have been told that Nero himself has sentenced you to die tomorrow during the great celebration in the arena."

Onesimus's thoughts were not of his impending death, but would he ever see Leah again. He thanked the prison guard for the water and lay back down, praying that God would provide a miracle of some kind.

# 25

The roar of the Romans could be heard at a great distance down the Tiber River. For thunderous was the applause, the stomping feet of thousands of impatient spectators in the arena.

The sight was in truth magnificent. The lower seats in the amphitheater, crowded with togas, were as white as snow. On the gilded podium sat Nero, wearing a jeweled collar and golden crown on his head. To his right sat Domitian, who had survived the superficial wound inflicted upon him by Leah. He was not dead as Leah had hoped. On both sides of Nero and Domitian were vestal virgins, great officials of the emperor's court, senators with embroidered togas, officers of the army with glittering weapons—in a word, all that was powerful, brilliant, and wealthy in Rome. Higher up, and surrounding the arena in colorful rows a sea of common heads, above which, from pillar to pillar hung festoons of roses, lilies, ivy, and grapevines.

People conversed loudly calling to each other and at times, broke into laughter at some witty word, and stomped their feet with impatience to hasten the spectacle.

Soon the stomping became like thunder and unbroken. Then when the shrill of trumpets was heard, there was a stillness of expectation of what was to come. Thousands of eyes were turned toward Nero who raised his handkerchief, a signal to begin the games.

All eyes were turned to the great iron gates, which a man approached amid the unusual silence. He struck the iron bars with a hammer, as if summoning to death those who were hidden behind them. Then both halves of the gate opened slowly, showing a black gully, out of which gladiators began to appear into the bright arena. They came in divisions of twenty-five, Thracians, Egyptians, Gauls, Persians, each nation separated, all heavily armed. At sight of them, here and there, rose applause, which soon turned into one eminence and unbroken storm.

From above and below were seen excited faces, clapping hands and open mouths, from which shouts burst forth. The gladiators circled the arena and then halted before the podium, proud, calm, and brilliant. Their salute was the stretching forth of their right hand upward, and raising their eyes and heads toward Nero.

Then they pushed apart quickly, occupying their places in the arena. They were to attack each other in whole detachments. During the contest, young patricians made enormous bets, often losing all they owned. The emperor bet, senators and praetorian guards bet, the populace bet. The audience took part in it with soul, heart, and eyes. They whistled, howled, roared, applauded, laughed, and urged on the combatants.

The gladiators in the arena fought with the rage of wild beasts; bodies were intertwined in a death grapple, strong limbs cracked in their joints, swords were buried in breasts, pale lips spat blood upon the sand. More and more naked bloody bodies lay stretched in death. The living fought upon the corpses, cutting their feet on broken weapons. The spectators intoxicated with death, drew into their lungs the exultation of it with ecstasy.

The conquered lay dead, almost every man. Only a few wounded knelt in the middle of the arena and, trembling, stretched their hands to the podium with a prayer for mercy from Nero. The winners were given rewards.

And then a moment of rest came, which at command of the all-powerful emperor, was turned into a feast. Cooling drinks were served, roasted meats and nuts, sweet cakes, wine, olives, and fruits. The people ate and drank, talked and milled about while the arena was cleared and new sand scattered about. When hunger and thirst was satisfied, hundreds of slaves bore baskets of gifts, from which they took various objects and threw them among the seats.

When lottery tickets were distributed, a battle began. People crowded, pushed, and sprang over seats trampling one another in a terrible crush, since whoever got the lucky number might win a house with a garden, a slave, or a wild beast, which could be sold back to the arena afterward. There was such disorder that frequently the praetorian guards had to interfere, and after every distribution, they carried out people with broken arms or legs.

Meanwhile, the trumpets announced the end of the interval. People began to leave the passageways where some had assembled. A general movement set in with the usual dispute about seats occupied previously. The uproar ceased after a time, and the Arena returned to order.

The sun had risen high, and its rays passed through the purple velum that covered the area where the elite sat, filling part of the arena with blood-colored light.

Now the perfect gave a sign, and the same old man who had called the gladiators to their death, walked slowly to the iron gate amid silence and struck three times on the door.

Throughout the arena was heard a deep murmur that grew louder with each chant; "The Christians! The Christians!" The iron gate creaked as it opened, but no one appeared. The spectators sensed something unusual was about to happen. What new way of slaughter of Christians had Nero thought of now.

The two guards who accompanied Onesimus, took off his chains, and out of the darkness walked Onesimus into the arena. The giant blinked his dark expressive eyes and placed his hand over them, for he was blinded by the brilliant sunlight. When his eyes drew accustom to the light, he slowly walked to the center of the arena. The crowd roared as he quickly scanned the rows of spectators, hoping to see Leah one last time before death.

In Rome, there was no lack of gladiators much larger than the common measure of a man, but Roman eyes had never seen the like of Onesimus. Nero, standing on the podium, seemed puny compared to this giant of a man. The crowd applauded with delight at his mighty limbs, his broad shoulders, and his arms of a Hercules. The murmur and applause became thunderous, for there could be no higher pleasure than to see those muscles in play in the exertion of a struggle.

He stood there, dressed only in a short tunic, naked from the waist up. He gazed at the spectators, now at Nero, now at the grating of the iron gate, where he thought his executioner would come.

From the moment he entered the arena, his simple heart was beating for the last time with the hope that perhaps a cross was waiting for him, but when he saw neither cross nor the hole in which it might be put, he thought he was unworthy of such favor—that he would find death another way. "If only I could see Leah one more time before I die," he reflected. "Surely, Priscilla and the others would take care of her."

He was unarmed and had determined to die as become a confessor of Christ the Lord, peacefully and patiently. So he knelt in the sand of the arena and, raising his eyes toward heaven, prayed.

This act displeased the spectators. They had had enough of those Christians in the past who died like sheep. They understood that if this giant of a man would not defend himself, the spectacle would be a failure. Here and there, hisses were heard. Some began to cry for scourgers, whose office it was to lash combatants unwilling to fight.

Nero, with a smirk on his face, knew something the spectators did not know; he knew that Onesimus would fight. In fact, they had not long to wait. Suddenly, at the motion of the emperor, the trumpets sounded.

Underneath the raised podium, a door opened and a girl was thrust out. Her white silk dress soiled, her beautiful copper-colored hair disheveled, and tears streaming down her face. The crowd, quiet for the moment, for many recognized this red-headed beauty who sang and danced in the streets of Rome and whose fame as Flamen was well known throughout the empire. She was captured and also charged with attempted murder of Domitian.

She surveyed the crowd and then saw Onesimus standing in the center of the arena with his mouth open. He could not believe what he was seeing. They ran to each other and embraced. When she looked up at his face, he bent down and kissed her tear stained lips. "I love you, Leah," he whispered softly.

Suddenly, another trumpet sounded and the spectators grew silent. The steel hinges creaked, as the iron gate opposite Nero's podium opened and into the arena charged a huge black German bull. His head and horns erect, prancing around the edge of the arena.

Mouths gasped in awe. The people rose from their seats as one man, for in the arena something uncommon was happening. The bull turned and faced Onesimus. He quickly placed Leah behind him and braced himself. The bull charged. Suddenly, the bull put on his breaks twenty feet from Onesimus. His hooves plowing into the sand, his haunches touching the ground, as he came to an abrupt stop. Slobbering at the mouth, he eye-balled Onesimus and began snorting and pawing the ground, flipping sand underneath him with his front hooves.

Onesimus knew he had to act quickly before the bull charged again. He quickly leaped forward just as the bull charged again. He grabbed the bull's horns and leaning forward with his legs braced behind him, the bull pushed him back. His feet plowed into the sand behind him. After being pushed back several feet, they came to a stand-still.

It seemed that the spectators ceased to breath. There was a deadly silence. People could not believe their eyes. Since Rome was Rome, no one had ever seen such a spectacle.

The Christian held the wild beast by the horns with his chest braced against the animal and his feet sinking deeper in the sand. His back was bent like a drawn bow, and the muscles in his arms came out so that the skin seemed to almost burst from the pressure, but Onesimus had stopped the bull in its tracks and the man and the beast remained so still that the spectators thought they were looking at a sculpture of stone.

Sweat poured from the body of Onesimus. The bull's body was curved so that it seemed a gigantic black ball. Which of the two would fail first, and which would fall first. That was the question for those spectators engrossed with these two struggling forces.

Nero himself stood up as well as the others. He had arranged this spectacle purposely, knowing of the strength of Onesimus. So they looked now with amazement, as if not believing that it could be real. Sweat covered the face of many, as if they themselves were struggling with the beast.

In the arena, nothing was heard save the sound of heavy breathing of the multitude. Their voices had died on their lips, but their hearts were beating in their breasts. It seemed to all that the struggle was lasting for ages. But the man and the beast continued on in their monstrous exertion.

It seemed as if the body of Onesimus was welded to that of the huge beast. Through eyes half blinded by perspiration which poured from his brow and, his body, he glanced back at Leah. She was beautiful even in the face of death. Her eyes were closed in prayer.

Her long fiery hair fell in front of her shoulders covering her breasts, as they rose and fell with her rapid breathing. Would God never allow them to become husband and wife. Words could not express their deep love for each other. "She must not die," he said to himself.

Straining, he managed to slowly slip his right hand under the mouth of the bull. With his left hand firmly pushing the bull's right horn to the left and with all the strength he could exert, he jerked the bull's nose up. He heard a crack, and the bull dropped to its knees and then rolled over on its side. He had broken the bull's neck.

Exhausted, he fell to his knees trembling. Leah ran to Onesimus and threw her arms around him, praising God for the miracle He had given them. The crowd roared with their approval. Standing and stomping, all raised their right hand with thumbs up, hoping Nero would do the same. For he alone had the power to give life (thumb up) or death (thumb down).

All eyes were on Nero who was frowning. He thrust out his arm, then raised his hand with his thumb pointed sideways. The crowd stomped and shouted with their thumbs high in the air. Their desire was for Nero to set them free. Nero's thumb began to dip down, then suddenly, his thumb turned upward, giving them life and freedom instead of death. The spectators went wild.

Two guards walked Onesimus and Leah back through the tunnel under the amphitheater and out the main gate to freedom. God's miracles still happen, they were thinking, as they made their way to Paul's house, which was the nearest place of refuge for them.

# PART V

# COLOSSE
## THE FORGIVEN FUGITIVE

# 26

Onesimus and Leah were unaware that Christians had gathered at Paul's house to pray for their deliverance. Upon their arrival, there was great joy and celebration that God had answered their prayer. Priscilla immediately took her shawl from her head and placed it upon Leah's half-naked body and took her to the bathing area in the house.

At the same time, many of the Christians were giving thanks and praising God for the miraculous deliverance of Onesimus and Leah from the jaws of death. Onesimus then shared with the group what they had just gone through. Luke took note of the dried blood, the bruises on the arms and chest of Onesimus, and insisted they go back to Luke's room for an examination. After several stitches to close up the gash in his head, he bathed and put on fresh clothes.

As they gathered back into the central room, Onesimus said to Paul, "I think God saved us for a purpose. And I believe that purpose is to share the gospel in Asia. I am deeply grateful to you and Luke for taking me in upon my arrival in Rome. You have been kind to me and have taught me much. And now if you would write that letter we talked about, I am ready to go back to Colosse and make things right with Philemon."

"When do you plan to leave?" Paul asked.

"As soon as possible," Onesimus answered. "But first, Leah and I would like to be married. Will you marry us?"

"Yes, I would be delighted to have that honor," Paul stated excitedly.

"I have just the dress for Leah to wear at her wedding," Priscilla stated. "And after the wedding, we will all have dinner at my house."

It was a happy group that visited well into the evening before parting. Leah spent the night with Priscilla, and the next day, they all met at Paul's house for the wedding.

It was a joyous group that celebrated the wedding. Timothy stood with Onesimus, and Priscilla with Leah, as the wedding was consummated. The group then moved to Aquila and Priscilla's house for the wedding meal, with toasts and well wishes being made for the couple. When the celebration ended, Onesimus and Leah spent their wedding night at Leah's rented house.

After Leah had bathed, she put on a robe and came into their bedchamber. She did not speak. Instead her eyes burned with much the same light of desire that moved Onesimus, and though she took not a step toward him, he knew that she was willingly his for the taking.

Slowly she reached up and removed the scarf of fine silk wrapped about her head. As she dropped the scarf to the rug on which she stood, her beautiful copper-colored hair fell past her shoulders. Her eyes were dark and luminous. The rich color of her cheeks needed no source from the cosmetic box of alabaster, nor the color of her full, moist lips demanding embellishment. Onesimus drew a deep breath and said hoarsely, "You are so beautiful."

She did not speak, but a smile parted her lips, revealing the pearly whiteness of her teeth and the moist pink tip of her tongue as it touched them for a second. Only when her fingers fumbled at the knot of the cord that bound the soft robe of almost transparent cloth, and he was forced to help her untie it, did he realize that she was in the grip of desire fully as great as his own.

Her fingers were trembling, and the touch of them upon his own was like fire. When the knot was finally loosened, she stepped back with a quick graceful movement and drew the robe aside to reveal that it was her only garment. Then she shrugged her shoulders and let it fall in a soft heap of fabric at her feet.

"My love! My own love!" Onesimus cried, knowing that at last he was to find the perfection of bliss he had never achieved before. As she stepped forward, Leah came into his arms, her body as eager as his own.

The next day, as promised, Paul wrote his letter to Philemon who was a wealthy member of the Colosse Church that met in his house. "I'm going to read to you the letter I wrote to Philemon. You need to know the content of it. It goes like this…"

> Paul, a prisoner of Jesus Christ, and Timothy, our brother. To Philemon, our beloved friend and fellow laborer, to the beloved Apphia, and Archippus, our fellow soldier, and to the church in your house. Grace to you and peace from God our Father and the Lord Jesus Christ.
>
> I thank my God, making mention of you always in my prayers, hearing of your love and faith which you have toward the Lord Jesus and toward all the saints, that the sharing of your faith may become effective by the acknowledgment of every good thing which is in you in Christ Jesus. For we have great joy and consolation in your love, because the hearts of the saints have been refreshed by you, brother.
>
> Therefore, though I might be very bold in Christ to command you what is fitting, yet for love's sake I rather appeal to you—being such a one as Paul, the aged, and also a prisoner of Jesus Christ—I appeal to you for my son, Onesimus, whom I have begotten while in my chains, who

once may have been unprofitable to you but now is useful
to you and to me.

I am sending him back. You therefore receive him, that
is, my own heart, whom I wish to keep with me, that on
your behalf he might minister to me for the gospel. But
without your consent I wanted to do nothing, that your
good deed might not be by compulsion, as it were, but
voluntary.

For perhaps he departed for a while for this purpose,
that you might receive him forever, no longer as a slave but
more than a slave—a beloved brother, especially to me but
how much more to you, both in the flesh and in the Lord.

If then you count me as a partner, receive him as you
would me. But if he has wronged you or owes anything,
put that on my account. I, Paul, am writing with my own
hand. I will repay—not to mention to you that you owe
me even your own self besides. Yes, brother, let me have joy
from you in the Lord; refresh my heart in the Lord.

Having confidence in your obedience, I write to you,
knowing that you will do even more than I say. But,
meanwhile, also prepare a guest room for me, for I trust
that through your prayers I shall be coming to you.

Epaphras, my fellow prisoner in Christ Jesus, greets
you, as do Mark, Aristarchus, Demas, Luke, and my fellow
laborers. The grace of our Lord Jesus Christ be with your
spirit. Amen.

After an evening of tearful good-byes, Onesimus and Leah,
along with Tychicus, who was to present the letter to Philemon,
began their journey to Colosse. At Puteoli, they boarded a ship
bound for Ephesus. Upon reaching Ephesus, they learned that
John, the youngest of the Apostles of Jesus and who was pastor
of the church at Ephesus, was banished to the Isle of Patmos for
preaching the gospel of Christ.

They then made their way from Ephesus to Colosse, and
then to Philemon's house. They were warmly greeted, especially

by Apphia, Philemon's wife. The letter from Paul was read by Tychicus and then given to Philemon. He looked at the letter, then slowly raising his head said to Onesimus, "I forgive you. Apphia and I have missed you. You will always be a son to us, and even more, now that you are a Christian. Welcome home." Having said that, he went to Onesimus and embraced him, and then Leah. He then called to one of his servants, "Kill a fatted calf, my son who was lost has come home. We shall have a feast and celebrate his return."

# 27

Meanwhile, back in Rome, Timothy suggested that he and Paul go to Velitrae and inquire about the welfare of Claudia Acte. On several occasions, Timothy had visited the modest village where the former mistress of Nero lived. He guided Paul there and Claudia Acte greeted them warmly, insisting that they spend the night before going back to Rome. Paul agreed and shortly they sat down to a delicious meal served in the triclinium of Acte's small villa. Only after the meal was finished and the dishes taken away and the two servants had retired to their quarters did she bring up the question of being spied upon.

"I am watched always," she explained as she shut the door to the triclinium, affording them privacy from eavesdropping. "We must be careful about anything we say outside this room."

"Do you think Nero has set spies to watch you?" Timothy asked.

"I'm sure of it. After Poppaea died, he asked me to become his concubine again, and when I refused, his pride was wounded. He could kill me at anytime but that wouldn't satisfy him. He must first find evidence that I am faithless. It isn't true, but there are those who might lie and testify against me, as did poor Octavia."

"We will leave early in the morning," said Paul. "My presence here must not be used against you."

"Rome still isn't safe for Christians," she warned. "You will be risking your life if you stay in Rome."

"The need here is greater than my desire to go to Spain. If it is Christ's will that I lay down my life in Rome, so be it," said Paul. "Can I do less than Peter and so many others were willing to do?"

For a while, it seemed that Paul might be able to inspire the Christians in Rome, though persecuted and in constant fear of death. In the vast network of galleries and connecting tunnels of the catacombs, many of them had been able to live with some hope of safety. But as the days passed, some began to voice openly the fear that Paul's presence might increase the danger to them, when their enemies learned that Paul was preaching Christ was Lord and not Nero. From that point on, it was but a step for one of the Roman Christians, his fear greater than his faith, to betray the apostle to the authorities.

Once again, Paul wore chains. This time, however, the fetters were heavy and his cell was located deep inside the praetorium. None dared help him except the faithful Luke who, because he served as physician to the praetorian guards, was allowed to enter the prison. As for Paul, he seemed almost to welcome imprisonment, and to Luke, it sometimes appeared that the apostle was actually courting death, for reasons which Luke suspected but which he did not voice.

The charges against the prisoner were first vague—merely those of being a Christian. But the citizens of Rome had long since been revolted by Nero's actions in persecuting those he had denounced falsely as the burners of Rome and of growing discontent throughout the empire over his excuses, his high taxes, and his misrule. So there was little real interest among the populace in any action against Paul. Besides, Rome was now being rebuilt in far greater beauty than ever before and some said openly that whoever set the fire to the city—whether Nero or the followers of Chrestus—had done its inhabitants a favor.

Knowing the sentiment among the people, Luke dared to hope Paul might be released. But then, a letter from prison to Timothy, Paul wrote: "I charge you before God and the Lord Jesus Christ, who will soon judge the living and the dead—I charge you by his appearing and his kingdom, to proclaim the tidings, to be urgent in season and out of season, to reprove, rebuke, exhort with all long suffering and doctrine."

The phrase "his kingdom" was only an expression of Paul's conviction that Christ's return was imminent. But to his enemies, who interpreted the letter, the mention of "Christ" and "kingdom" together were the final proof of treason they needed to condemn the apostle. On this charge, proceedings were set in motion to try him for that crime.

The final proof of Luke's assumption concerning Paul's real reason for staying in Rome came, when the apostle wrote near the end of the letter to Timothy: "I am now ready to be offered and the time of my departure is at hand, I have fought a good fight. I have finished my course. I have kept the faith. Henceforth, there is laid up for me a crown of righteousness which the Lord, the righteous judge, shall give me at that day. And not to me only but to all who love his appearing."

Reading the words, Luke realized that Paul was writing his own epitaph. During the years since the vision before Demascus, the apostle had labored steadily toward the day when he would face the Lord in glory and whether Paul saw Christ in person at His coming, or went proudly to meet Him through the gates of death, made little difference now. He would be wearing in his own words, "The whole armor of God," including "the shield of faith and the sword of the spirit."

With what they considered a valid charge, the magistrates of Rome moved with unusual swiftness. A colorful assembly gathered in one of the great basilicas standing in the Forum, the very heart of Rome. Nero presided from a platform at one end of the rectangular building, down whose center was an isle with seats on either side. Upon the platform stood the ivory chair of the magistrate, and behind him was arrayed the council of assessors, experts in Roman law. But Nero's justice—if it could be called that—was embodied only in himself.

An open space was provided before the magistrate for the prisoner and those who defended him, as well as his accusers. The rest of the basilica was open to the public who filled it and spilled out into the streets around it.

Paul had forbidden his associates to appear at his trial as witnesses on his behalf, knowing that by doing so they would only be convicting themselves. He stood alone as his own defender, calling only one witness, Luke, who was reasonably safe from prosecution, to prove his innocence of the first charge against him, namely that he was one of the Christians who had participated in the burning of Rome. Luke quickly proved that Paul had been freed by the Imperial Court of the previous charge against him.

To the second charge of giving allegiance to a man who claimed to be more powerful than the emperor and Rome itself, Paul made the ringing defense that Jesus, being God, was indeed above any earthly ruler and that allegiance to Him was no more treasonous than the allegiance given by Romans to Apollo, Zeus, and other gods.

Finally, as he had once written to Timothy, Paul summed up in the fewest possible words, the very nature of Christ with these word: "God was manifest in the flesh, justified in the spirit; beheld by angels, preached among the Gentiles; believed on in the world, received up in glory."

"The Chrestus you worship was a man," Nero said. "Do you claim that he was also God?"

"He was and is God made man, for the salvation of men," said Paul.

"Do you also say that Chrestus will return to earth to judge the living and the dead?"

"I have preached that doctrine from the day I began to serve Him," Paul said proudly and a murmur ran through the vast basilica for, in their eyes, he had condemned himself of the charge of treason.

"If you say that Chrestus will judge, when none can judge in Rome except by the authority of the emperor, then your allegiance to him must be above your allegiance to the emperor," said Nero.

Paul lifted his head and his voice was clear as he repeated the words that sealed his doom: "Christ is God, manifest in the flesh, justified in the spirit, beheld by angels, preached among the Gentiles, believed on in the world, and received up in glory."

"Have you any other defense?" Nero asked.

"I proclaim my loyalty to Caesar and to Rome in earthly matters," said Paul. "But in things concerning the Spirit and God, my allegiance is to Christ."

"You have condemned yourself out of your own mouth," said Nero, ending the hearing. "I sentence you to death by the ax."

# 28

The Roman senate had long ago imposed an ordinance of Roman citizens requiring ten days to elapse between the sentence of the court in a capital crime and its execution, giving the emperor time to consider the case and, if he chose to be merciful, remit the sentence. In Paul's case, there was no remission and ten days after the trial, a small procession left the city by way of the Ostian Gate.

A centurion commanded the detail of the praetorian guard that marched on either side of the prisoner, whose ankle chains had been removed so he could walk. Behind him was the headsman, bearing the ax which, for Roman citizens, was considered a more merciful form of execution than crucifixion normally reserved for slaves and for despicable criminals.

Only Luke, of all the apostle's companions, accompanied him on his last journey. A rabble of jeering Romans, eager to see a man meet his death, followed the small procession. Just beyond the Ostian Gate, they passed the pyramid of Caius Cestius and almost a mile farther, came to a narrow lane leading down to a hollow surrounded by low hills forming a small natural amphitheater. Known as Aquae Salviae, it was a frequent site of executions.

Watching from the edge of the crowd gathered in the little hollow where the drama of death was taking place, Luke saw—through the tears that filled his eyes—Paul step forward to the wooden block in the center. The apostle's head was proudly erect and his shoulders straight, as if he were wearing the invisible armor of God, to which he had so often referred.

When Paul's lips moved, the words he spoke were no request for mercy or even pity. Rather they had been spoken long ago by another man on the eve of his own death and repeated to Luke by Paul himself, the words of Stephen when he had said, as the apostle did now: "Behold, I see the heavens opened and the Son of Man standing on the right hand of God!"

The centurion in charge of the detail carrying out the execution stepped forward with a blindfold for the doomed man's eyes, but Paul shook his head and moved directly to the block. Standing there, he looked up at the sky and Luke saw a smile on his face, a smile so radiant that even the babble of onlookers was stilled in wonder. The headsman reached out his hand to shove Paul to his knees, but before he could touch the broad shoulders that had for so long borne proudly the armor of God, the apostle knelt before the block.

Watching as the heavy-bladed ax was raised high, Luke could not help crying out in wonder, as did many others among the onlookers. For the shadow of the falling blade was suddenly blotted out by a blinding glory that shone around the kneeling man.

# 29

I t was summer by the time Timothy reached Ephesus. Leaving Luke and others in Rome, he had come to bring the news of Paul's death to the churches in Asia. After speaking to the church at Ephesus and requesting that they spread the news, he traveled to Colosse.

One look at Timothy's face told Onesimus that his friend had brought grave tidings indeed, for Timothy seemed to have aged a dozen years in the months since he had left him in Rome.

"Paul is dead," Timothy said softly.

There was hushed silence for a moment and then Philemon, with tears in his eyes spoke. "Paul was the greatest human being I have ever known. It was because of him that me and my family now have the hope of heaven, and when God is ready, we too shall see him again."

"Paul took me in and taught me everything I know about Christ," Onesimus stated as tears rolled down his face. "He gave his life for the faith that we must carry on."

"The church at Ephesus has asked me to be their pastor, and I have accepted," Timothy stated. "The Apostle John, their former pastor, has been banished to the Isle of Patmos and may never return. There is much work to be done. I trust that God will lay on your heart the place He has for you to serve, Onesimus."

"Leah and I have been praying that God would show us where He wants us to serve. Philemon has been kind enough to allow us to stay with him until God shows us the way He wants us to go."

"There were Christians from Berea at the church in Ephesus inquiring about a pastor for their church. Perhaps you should pray about it and see if God impresses you to go talk to those people. God may want you to serve him there."

Timothy spent the night in the house of Philemon and left the next day for Ephesus. Onesimus and Leah headed for Berea. There they talked with the elders of the church who were very much impressed with the couple. Onesimus spoke to the congregation, and after much prayer, they asked him to be their pastor. Onesimus felt this was God's call for him to serve, and he accepted their invitation to become their pastor.

The people of Berea were overjoyed to have this fine couple serve as spiritual leaders of their church.

And so it was, that Onesimus whose name means useful, was a runaway slave. But who was saved by the grace of God, and came home as a forgiven fugitive, married to the love of his life, and lived happily serving Christ for the rest of his life.

# A Closing Word

Timothy took letters Paul wrote to him back to the church of Ephesus and became pastor after John's banishment to the Isle of Patmos. His mother Eunice and grandmother Lois moved from Lystra to Ephesus to be with him.

Mark, being the interpreter of Peter, wrote exactly whatever he remembered of Peter's teaching, which became the Gospel of Mark in the New Testament. He labored ultimately as pastor of the church he established in Alexandria.

Luke, the blessed physician, was the friend, care giver, and companion of the Apostle Paul. And from his notes of Paul's teaching, the Gospel of Luke was born, as well as the Acts of the Apostles. These writings were taken to the churches of Asia. Luke remained in Rome helping persecuted Christians until his death.

Aquila and Priscilla were banished from Rome by Claudius. They became zealous promoters of Christ in Asia. Aquila became the bishop of Heraclea, and today, a festival is named in their honor.

Onesimus of Perga and Leah of Petra, raised a beautiful red-haired daughter who looked just like her mother. Leah taught music in Berea, and Onesimus preached and ministered to the people of that region, where they spent the rest of their life serving God.

Nero committed suicide in 69 AD. Ten years later, Domitian became the emperor of Rome in 79 AD. The persecution of Christians continued.

Again, I repeat. To those who read this book, it is my sincere prayer that the times, places, and the people of the first century AD may come alive for them as they have for me. And that they, too, may come to know Jesus Christ, the Risen Lord, as did my friend, Onesimus, the forgiven fugitive.

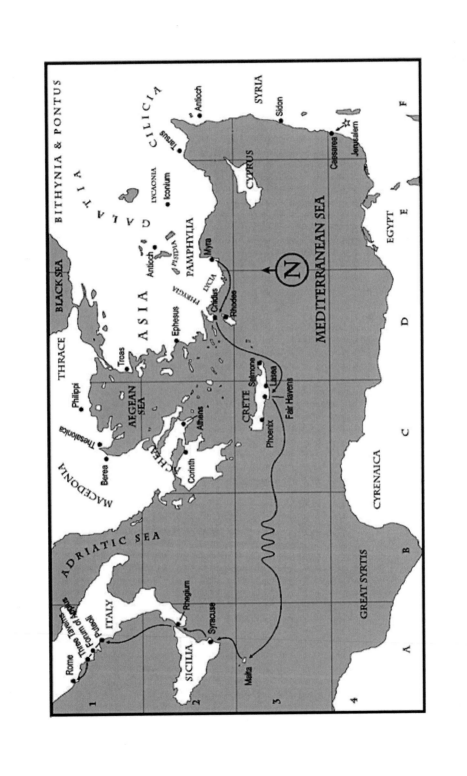